"Must you work without your shirt? It's so . . . coarse."

Judd stared at her blankly. "Just what is it about my bare chest that bothers you?"

"It's just too . . . too . . . bare." Ginger flushed hotly.

"While we're on the subject of bare, let's talk about those shorts."

"There is nothing wrong with these shorts!"

"Either those shorts are too short, or your legs are too long." His eyes were the color of hot, melted metal, and Ginger felt a fire begin to burn within her.

She reached up to touch his chest, wanting to test her power—but before her hand could touch him, he grabbed her wrist.

"What's your game, Ginger?" His voice was a tightly controlled growl. "Do you want to see how far you can push me? If I find you desirable?" He grabbed her hips, and pressed her close to him. "Don't play the tease with me," he said between clenched teeth. "You're out of your league."

Dear Reader,

August is vacation month, and no matter where you're planning to go, don't forget to take along this month's Silhouette Romance novels. They're the perfect summertime read! And even if you can't get away, you can still escape from it all for a few hours of love and adventure with Silhouette Romance books.

August continues our WRITTEN IN THE STARS series. Each month in 1992 we're proud to present a book that focuses on the hero and his astrological sign. This month we're featuring the proud, passionate Leo man in Suzanne Carey's intensely emotional *Baby Swap*.

You won't want to miss the rest of our fabulous August lineup. We have love stories by Elizabeth August, Brittany Young, Carol Grace and Carla Cassidy. As a special treat, we're introducing a talented newcomer, Sandra Paul. And in months to come, watch for Silhouette Romance novels by many more of your favorite authors, including Diana Palmer, Annette Broadrick and Marie Ferrarella.

The Silhouette Romance authors and editors love to hear from readers and we'd love to hear from *you*.

Happy reading from all of us at Silhouette!

Valerie Susan Hayward
Senior Editor

CARLA CASSIDY

Fire and Spice

Published by Silhouette Books New York

America's Publisher of Contemporary Romance

To the memory of Grandpa Cook,
who taught me to love the land

SILHOUETTE BOOKS
300 E. 42nd St., New York, N.Y. 10017

FIRE AND SPICE

Copyright © 1992 by Carla Bracale

ISBN: 0-373-08884-1

First Silhouette Books printing August 1992

Printed in the U.S.A.

Books by Carla Cassidy

Silhouette Romance

Patchwork Family #818
Whatever Alex Wants... #856
Fire and Spice #884

CARLA CASSIDY

is the author of ten young adult novels. She's been a cheerleader for the Kansas City Chiefs football team and has traveled the East Coast as a singer and dancer in a band, but the greatest pleasure she's had is in creating romance and happiness for readers.

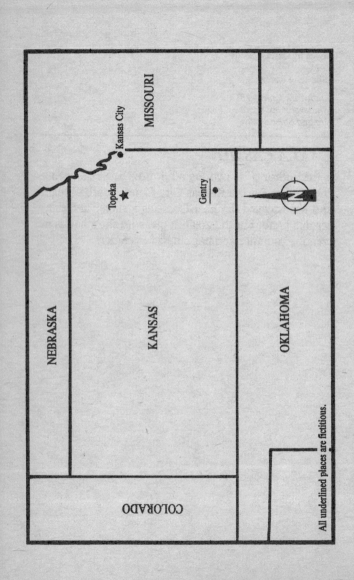

All underlined places are fictitious.

Chapter One

Ginger Taylor knew the reading of a will was supposed to be a solemn occasion, but for the life of her, she couldn't control the giggles that threatened to burst out of her. She bit her bottom lip, dug her nails into her palms, even tried staring at a spot on the wall in an effort to control the attack she felt coming.

It had always been this way. Whenever she was nervous, frightened or upset, she got the giggles. At the moment she was all three, and the nervous laughter threatened to erupt out of her.

She shifted uncomfortably in the stiff-backed wooden chair, wishing she'd had a chance to freshen up after her trip before coming directly to Mr. Roberts' office. But a broken fan belt in Indiana had made the twenty-four-hour trip from New York City to

Gentry, Kansas a thirty-eight-hour drive, getting her to town just in time for the appointment at the lawyer's office. She turned in her chair as the door behind her opened and Mr. Roberts stuck his head in. "We'll be ready to begin in just a few minutes. We're just waiting for Mr. Bishop to arrive."

"Mr. Bishop?" Ginger felt the blood drain from her face, and all impulse to laugh died. "Judd Bishop?"

Mr. Roberts nodded. "He called just a few moments ago and said he's on his way. As soon as he arrives, we'll proceed."

When Mr. Roberts disappeared out the door again, the pleasant expression on Ginger's face turned to a glower. Judd Bishop. She'd hoped that by this time the wind would have blown him back to wherever it was he had come from ten years before. She'd hoped a black hole had opened up beneath his feet and swallowed him up. No, that wouldn't have been final enough, for Judd would only have given Mother Earth indigestion, and she would have belched him back up again.

It had been a black day years ago when Judd Bishop had shown up in his rattletrap pickup, looking for a job on the farm. He'd wheedled his way into her grandfather's heart. It had been Judd's presence that had made it impossible for Ginger to remain at the farm.

"Oh, Grandpa," she breathed tremulously, still unable to believe that he was gone. The heart attack had been so sudden, so final. If only she'd known it would all end this way, that she wouldn't have a chance to tell her grandpa goodbye. If she'd only known what the future held, she would never have left the farm years ago. If only Judd Bishop had never entered their lives. But all the *if only*s in the world couldn't change the fact that her grandfather was dead and she hadn't even been notified in time to attend the funeral. She had yet to cry. Crying was something she had never done easily.

She turned once again at the sound of the door opening. He filled the doorway with his broad shoulders, seeming to suck all the air out of the small room with his very presence. Judd Bishop—she'd forgotten how overwhelmingly masculine he was with his twilight eyes and bold features. His dark hair was longer than she remembered, but the memory of his mocking lips was burned into her brain. She snapped her head back around, not wanting to look at him, not able to pretend civility.

"Well, well." The familiar, rough-textured voice rolled over her, evoking memories better left untapped. He walked around her and sat down at the table directly across from her. "You cut your hair," he observed.

Her hand unconsciously went up to smooth the russet-colored curls atop her head. She still was not used to the lack of the thick weight of hair on her neck.

Judd grinned, the mocking smile that had always made her teeth ache. He leaned across the table, his

warm breath fanning her face, bringing with it the tang
of mint and a fresh scent that reminded her of a field
of wheat during a summer rainstorm. "You can cut it,
curl it, crimp it and style it, but it will always be paprika to me."

At the mention of the hated nickname, she stiffened, scathing words boiling to her tongue.

Mr. Roberts entered the room, forcing her to swallow her angry retort. She settled for the look of cool
disdain she'd practiced for so many hours in front of
her mirror during her years away.

Mr. Roberts set his attaché case on the table,
punched the horn-rimmed glasses up firmly on his
nose and drew a pen from the pocket protector attached to his crisp, white shirt. "Now, your grandfather's will is fairly straightforward, except for one
area. I think it best if I just read it, then answer any
questions you might have." The lawyer cleared his
throat and pulled several sheets of paper from the attaché case.

As he began to read, Ginger was able to forget the
disturbing presence of the man across from her. She
closed her eyes for a moment, listening to her grandfather's final wishes, filled with sorrow that she hadn't
been there to tell him goodbye, tell him how much she
loved him. She breathed a sigh of relief as Mr. Roberts read her grandfather's bequest to her. Serenity was
hers. Her grandfather had known how much she loved
the farm. He'd been the one responsible for teaching
her to respect the fertile fields, revere the continuity of

nature's cycles. From the time Ginger had been five years old, not a day had passed that Tom Taylor hadn't taken his granddaughter by the hand and shown her one of nature's little miracles happening on the farm. It could have been something as minute as a gauzy spider's web, forming on the steering wheel of the tractor, or something as awe inspiring as an entire field of golden winter wheat, moving in waves like the sea in response to a spring wind. Those were the times most dear to Ginger's heart, and those were the times she'd missed most when Judd had usurped her place with her grandfather.

You're history now, bud, she thought, looking at the man sitting across from her. *The first act I will perform as the owner of Serenity is to send you packing.* Even as this thought entered her mind, she couldn't help but notice that the years had done nothing to diminish his sinful attractiveness. Irritation swept through her, and a smug smile curved her lips as she fantasized the way he'd look when she fired him. However, as the words Mr. Roberts had just finished reading penetrated, her smug smile transformed to a look of utter horror.

"There must be some mistake," she said, staring at the lawyer in disbelief. "That last part, it can't be right."

"I'm sorry, Ginger, but it was your grandfather's wish that Mr. Bishop remain at the farm as foreman for as long as he desires."

"And I'll probably desire to stay forever." Judd smiled, a tight-lipped one that had nothing to do with humor.

Ginger returned her attention to Mr. Roberts. "There must be a loophole. What about the part concerning living elsewhere? Surely that can be changed."

Mr. Roberts shook his head. "The terms of the will are quite specific. In the next year, should you decide to live anyplace other than at Serenity, then the farm is to be sold. If for any reason, in the next year, Mr. Bishop should decide to live elsewhere, then his position as foreman is terminated. The only way your hands are tied is in the fact that you cannot fire Mr. Bishop. If he leaves, then it must be of his own volition."

Ginger stared down at her hands, refusing to look at Judd, not wanting to see any triumph that might be there in his dark gray eyes. Damn him. How had he done it? How had Judd managed to influence her grandfather into assuring him a position at the farm forever? Six years . . . of course, he'd had six years in which to wheedle and cajole, trick and manipulate an old man.

Before she had a chance to assimilate these thoughts, Judd stood up. "If we're finished here, I have work to do."

"Yes, of course." Mr. Roberts also stood up, shaking the hand Judd held out to him. Ginger stared down at the table top, aware of Judd's gaze on her. She didn't want to look at him, she didn't want her anger to get in the way of her thought process. And she definitely needed to think.

"I guess I'll see you out at the farm, Boss Lady." The title rolled off his tongue with the smoothness of hot buttered rum on a wintry night.

She looked up at him and nodded stiffly, refusing to allow him to crawl under her skin. She knew if she allowed him to lodge there, he'd become as irritating as a chigger, itching and aggravating until she ended up doing something stupid. That's what had happened six years before when in a childish temper tantrum she'd packed up and left. Well, he wouldn't goad her into losing her temper. She was no longer an undisciplined, uncontrollable eighteen-year-old. She was almost twenty-four years old, and she needed to remain coolheaded and alert.

She met his gaze levelly, refusing to rise to the challenge his seemed to hold. She sighed with relief as he was the one to turn away, stalking out of the room, which seemed to fill once again with light and space.

"Now, your grandfather left this portfolio of information for you," Mr. Roberts explained once Judd was gone. He pulled a stapled group of papers out and handed them to Ginger. "This should explain what kind of financial arrangements your grandfather had with Mr. Bishop and the rest of the farm help. It also contains a complete list of assets and debts, summing up your grandfather's financial status at the time of his death. As you can see, your grandfather left you a relatively wealthy woman."

"Yes, well, before we get into details on all this, there is something I'd like you to do for me."

"Certainly, you know I'm at your disposal, Ginger," Mr. Roberts said, his voice heavy with deference.

Ginger leaned forward on the table, eyeing the lawyer with determination. "You and I are going to put our heads together and find a legal loophole I can climb through to get rid of that insufferable man, Judd Bishop."

Judd rolled down the window of the pickup and rested his arm along the door molding, allowing the warm, mid-morning breeze to caress the dark hairs on his forearm.

The pickup truck was the same one that had carried him to Serenity ten years before. Ten years…where had the time gone? He'd arrived at the farm a scared nineteen-year-old, wondering at his welcome, wondering if he'd ever find a place where he felt he belonged. He'd found his own little piece of Heaven at Serenity. But if the Garden of Eden had a serpent, he could bet that snake would have hair the color of paprika.

Ginger. He smiled and shook his head thoughtfully. He wouldn't have recognized her if not for her hair. When she'd left Serenity six years before, she'd been a long-legged, tangle-haired hellion, spitting curses that would have made a sailor blush. Six years in New York had smoothed the edges, polished the rough-cut stone.

Funny, for a moment there in the lawyer's office he'd thought he was going to be able to get a rise out of her. He'd seen the crackle of fire in her cinnamon-colored eyes, almost smelled the sulfur of hell's fire and brimstone about to erupt, but it hadn't happened. He'd almost been sorry.

Initially, when Ginger had packed up and left the farm, Tom had been devastated. Then he'd learned that Ginger had gone to live with her great-aunt Loretta, and Tom had hoped that his sister would be able to corral some of Ginger's spirit. The old man would spin around in his grave if he thought Ginger's spirit had been broken.

Judd's heart constricted at thoughts of Tom Taylor. The man had been more than boss and mentor to Judd. He'd been a friend and a father figure. He'd made Judd feel important. He'd taught Judd how to love.

The old man had been true, too. From the time Judd had been a young boy, Tom had promised there would always be a place for him at Serenity. In death, Tom had sealed that promise by legally assuring him a job at the farm for as long as Judd wanted it.

And that meant Judd now had to fulfill the promise he'd made to Tom. Judd couldn't believe he'd actually promised the old man that he'd find a good husband for Ginger. Linden Hammonds...the name popped into his head unbidden. Linden was a nice young man. He frowned. *Too* nice ... Ginger would chew up the amenable Linden and spit him out. Judd mentally scratched Linden's name off the top of his imaginary list. He sighed. Surely in the town of Gentry and the surrounding area he could find someone who was man enough for Ms. Ginger Taylor.

Murder was out. Mr. Roberts managed to convince her that the murder of Judd Bishop was an illogical solution to the problem. In truth, there seemed to be no solution to the problem.

Ginger left Mr. Roberts's office discouraged. It was devastating to think of living at the farm without the presence of her grandfather. But it was a nightmare come true to realize she was going to have to share her space with Judd.

She got into her car and headed for home. Yes, Serenity had been home for as long as she could remember. She'd been three when a car accident had taken her parents and she'd been sent to the farm. She didn't remember any life before she'd come to Serenity. It had become her world, encompassing her in security and love. The last six years in New York had only assured her that the farm was where her happiness lay. Her Aunt Loretta had been wonderful, introducing Ginger to new concepts, giving her the woman's touch that had been missing from Ginger's life since the death of her grandmother when Ginger was ten. But in the midst of all the shopping trips, the beauty shop appointments, the cultural events, even Aunt Loretta had recognized that a piece of Ginger's heart was locked away, unmoved by anything the big city had to offer. Ginger had been like a jigsaw puzzle, with an integral center piece missing.

As she turned the car down the tree-lined lane, driving beneath the tall wooden entrance that read Serenity, she felt that missing piece locking into place, and for the first time in years she felt whole and at peace. She was home.

She pulled her car up and parked in front of the large, white, three-story farmhouse. She climbed out of the car, frowning as she saw how badly the house needed painting, the tangled growth of weeds and flowers where once carefully tended flower beds had been. There was an air of neglect about the place, like a lover suddenly abandoned and left, forlorn and in despair.

She leaned against the car, her eyes narrowed in thought. This kind of maintenance was part of Judd's job here. He was being paid not only a handsome salary, but a share of the farm's profits as well. He'd probably found her grandfather an easy taskmaster. But there was a new ballgame now, with a new umpire, and she'd see to it that the farm was not neglected due to laziness. Stipulation or not, Judd Bishop sure as hell wasn't going to take advantage of her.

"Ginger? Is that you?"

She turned at the deep, familiar voice, her face lighting up at the sight of the huge man standing awkwardly by the edge of the barn.

"It's me, Ray." She hesitated only a moment, then ran over to where he stood, throwing her arms around his massive shoulders and giving him a smacking kiss on the cheek. He blushed the same vivid color as his red T-shirt. "Oh, Ray, it's so good to be home."

She stepped back and eyed him critically, thrilled to see that he hadn't changed. At forty years old, Ray Colton had the weathered face of a man ten years older. But it was the face of a kind, gentle man. "It's good to see some things stay the same, like the fact that you still look like you need a shave and your favorite food is Lisa's pies." She gave him a fond pat on his broad belly. "How is Lisa? I've missed her."

He pointed a finger toward the house. "She's inside, waiting for you." Ginger nodded and turned toward the house, pausing as the big man said her name once again. "It's good to have you back," he grunted, his face still colored deeply. "Things haven't been the same around here since you left. We missed you."

Ginger smiled warmly, knowing how difficult words of emotion were for the man who'd been like a favorite uncle. She turned and ran back to the house, anxious now to get settled and unpacked, see all the people she'd missed, feel the permanence of being finally home.

She went inside, walking with hesitant steps through the living room and into the kitchen. Lisa was there, her back to Ginger, pouring a cup of coffee.

"Lisa." Ginger smiled as the woman whirled around. Ginger's eyes widened as she saw the protrusion of Lisa's stomach. "Lisa…how…when?" Ginger sputtered in happy surprise.

Lisa laughed in delight and rubbed her hand across the expanse of her big belly. "I'd think after six years in the big city, you'd know the how. As to when, I'm due in about two months."

"Oh Lisa, that's wonderful." The two women hugged, then stepped back and eyed each other.

"I know it's crazy. We tried so hard for so long we'd given up. Needless to say, Ray and I are thrilled. It's what we've wanted for so long." Lisa smiled, her face glowing with happiness. "Now, let me get a good look at you. If it wasn't for that hair and those copper eyes, I'm not sure I would have recognized you. No scabby knees, no dirt smudges on your face. I guess you've finally grown up."

"And you've definitely grown out," Ginger laughed, patting Lisa's stomach as she had Lisa's husband's only moments before.

"Sit down, honey. I was just pouring myself a cup of coffee, and I'll pour you one, too. I want to hear everything that's transpired in your life over the past six years."

For the next hour, Ginger filled Lisa in on her time away from the farm. She told her about attending the theater, the opera, the many charity events her aunt was involved in. Lisa listened with rapt attention. At thirty-seven years old, Lisa had never been farther away from Gentry than the neighboring town of Pittsburgh.

"It all sounds so wonderful," Lisa breathed when Ginger had related all she thought would interest the older woman. "But I never really understood exactly why you left. It all happened so suddenly, one day you were here and the next day you were on your way to New York. What happened?"

Ginger's eyes darkened as she thought back in time. "Let's just say I got tired of some of the company around here. I decided to leave before I did something stupid."

Lisa's blue eyes sparkled humorously. "I heard about your driving the tractor through the side of the barn. I know you poured a jar of molasses into Judd's underwear drawer, too. Sweetie, you weren't exactly a model of decorum before you left."

"Yeah, well, I had to get away," Ginger replied, her eyes flickering like the warning distant lightning before a summer storm. "But I'll tell you this much—the next time somebody packs their bags and leaves here, it's not going to be me."

"Are you expecting somebody to leave? I guess you're talking about Judd." Lisa sighed. "I guess that means your attitude toward him hasn't changed. I was hoping . . ." Her voice trailed off.

"Hoping what? That my attitude toward him should undergo a complete transformation? That while I was away my feelings for him would soften and mellow out?" She snorted. "Not likely. The only way I'll feel a modicum of affection for Mr. Judd Bishop is if he left this place and went to live on a deserted island in the Caribbean where I would never have to look at him or hear his voice again—" She broke off, feeling the old familiar stirring of anger Judd had always been able to evoke.

Lisa shook her head in bewilderment. "I've never understood the animosity between the two of you. If I didn't know better I'd swear..." She didn't finish the thought aloud. Instead, she stood up and took her cup to the sink. "There's something I'd like to ask you," she said, rinsing out the cup then turning around to face Ginger. "For the past several months, your grandfather and Judd had been paying me to kind of keep the house clean and cook the meals." She smiled sheepishly. "It was a little extra money I was socking away for the baby. Anyway, I was just wondering if maybe you'd be interested in keeping me on."

Although the question was asked with seeming nonchalance, Ginger heard a tad of desperation in Lisa's voice. She had a sudden recollection of whispered rumors of the financial problems of the couple...the lingering illness of Ray's father, debts left by overwhelming hospital bills.

Ginger got up from the table and put her cup in the sink, then laid a hand on Lisa's arm. "I'm so relieved that you made the offer. I've been wondering how I was ever going to be able to see the running of the farm and the cooking and housekeeping. Why don't we just keep the same arrangement you had with Grandfather?''

"Sure, that's just fine by me." Lisa was unable to hide her obvious relief. "Now, I'm going to get out of here and let you get unpacked and settled in." She looked at her wristwatch, then back at Ginger. "The way we've been working it is that I come about five in the mornings and fix breakfast. I go home right after noon, then come back around four to start on dinner.''

"That sounds just fine," Ginger assured her, walking with her to the back door. "I just hope you don't walk back and forth, traipsing across the field.''

"Oh no," Lisa laughed. "Ray has me using the car. That man won't even let me walk to the mailbox and back." She smiled at Ginger and started through the door, but paused and turned back. "Ginger, try to go easy on Judd. He's been the glue that's held us together these last couple of days.''

Right, Ginger thought moments later as she went out to her car to retrieve her suitcases. Judd was the glue that had held everything together, everything except her. He'd made all the arrangements for the funeral without her. Hell, he'd gotten in touch with her so late, she'd missed the funeral.

As she unpacked in her childhood bedroom, her thoughts continued along the same vein. She could remember the first day her animosity toward Judd had appeared. She'd been almost thirteen years old, and it was the first time her grandfather had said, "Run along and find something to do, Ginger. Judd and I are talking." Those words soon became a familiar refrain. Tom, who had always been Ginger's companion and best friend, suddenly had a new companion and friend. Ginger had responded with the hurt bewilderment of a pubescent girl, and she decided at that time that she wouldn't be satisfied until Judd Bishop was gone. Unfortunately she'd been the one who'd eventually left.

Now her grandfather was gone and she was left with the farm and an unbendable will that provided Judd a piece of Serenity for as long as he wanted. She wanted him out. He didn't belong here. He wasn't part of the family, he was an interloper who had wormed his way into a cushy job and a big paycheck.

She went to her bedroom window and stared out. The afternoon breeze stirred the yellow gingham curtains, bringing with it the scent of warm sunshine on fertile fields, freshly mowed grass, winter wheat bursting with ripeness. It was the smell of home, and Ginger wasn't about to share the rest of her life with an obnoxious, mocking, insensitive clod like Judd Bishop.

She smiled, pulling on her lower lip thoughtfully. Judd had made it clear he wanted to stay on, but would he be so eager to remain if Serenity became synonymous with hell?

Chapter Two

Ginger decided to try a little rational negotiation first. She finished unpacking, changed into a pair of cutoffs and a T-shirt, then headed out to find Judd.

Ray told her that Judd was down in the cow pasture by the pond mending a stretch of barbed wire fencing, so she headed in that direction.

She was in no hurry, finding the sun warm and pleasing on her back and enjoying reacquainting herself with her home.

She followed the lane that led her past the barn, stepping carefully across the metal cattle guard and into the meadow where cattle were grazing. As she passed, one of the straw-colored Charolais heifers mooed in greeting. Oh, she'd missed it all so much—the lowing of the cattle, the hum of the cicadas at dusk, the mechanical hum of combines in the distance.

Her footsteps slowed as she crested a ridge and spotted Judd, working on a section of fencing next to a large cattle trough. His back was to her and she paused, taking the opportunity to gather her thoughts before confronting him.

She would be cool and controlled, she thought, watching him swing a sledge hammer around over his head and down on the top of a wooden post with deadly accuracy. She would not lose her temper no matter how he baited her.

She watched in fascination as Judd swung the hammer once again, causing the muscles of his back and shoulders to expand and bulge with the effort. His shirtless torso was the deep bronze of a man accustomed to working outside without benefit of cover.

It was amazing how the sunlight seemed to love his hair, dancing on the darkness to pull out subtle shades of deep auburn. It was equally amazing the way he could move with such grace and agility considering the fact that his worn jeans hugged his slender hips and taut buttocks with a tightness that should be deemed obscene.

"You going to stand there gawking all afternoon or is there something in particular you wanted?" He spoke without turning around, making her flush with irritation as she realized where her thoughts had been headed.

"I need to talk to you." She walked over to stand directly behind him, watching as his hands worked with deftness to connect a piece of the barbed wire fencing to the post.

"About what?"

"About the will . . . about you remaining here."

He stopped what he was doing and turned to face her, his gray eyes holding the mocking amusement she'd always found so infuriating.

"What's to discuss? I'm here and I'm going to remain here."

"I thought maybe you'd be interested in negotiating some kind of deal," she offered tentatively.

He crossed his arms in front of him and leaned back against the post, dark eyebrows quirked with interest. "Deal? What, exactly do you have in mind?"

"I was thinking maybe we could come to some sort of financial agreement." Ginger began to pace back and forth in front of him, encouraged by the mere fact that he was willing to listen. "I realize you've invested ten years of your life working here at the farm, and Grandpa's will left you in the enviable position of having job security virtually for the rest of your life." She stopped pacing and looked at him. "It's sort of like you have a contract, and I'm willing to buy it out. I'll compensate you for the time it will take you to relocate."

"Sounds fascinating," he observed, his expression enigmatic. "Please continue. What kind of compensation are we talking about?"

Ginger felt a flare of triumph surge through her. She'd suspected all along that Judd didn't really care about Serenity itself, that on that day ten years earlier when he'd pulled in looking for a job he'd smelled an easy mark. An old man with no living relative except a fourteen-year-old granddaughter...what a setup for a drifter who had nothing.

She named a figure. When there was no response, no flicker of expression on his face, she named a higher figure, then held her breath.

"Very interesting." He shook his head as if contemplating the offer. "Now, let me make you a counter offer. I'll buy the farm from you and you can go back to New York and attend all those fancy theater openings and parties you wrote your grandpa about."

"You read my letters?" Ginger's voice was a squeak of outrage.

Judd shrugged. "Tom's eyesight wasn't so good. He often had me read him the mail. Besides—" he grinned once again "—they weren't exactly filled with national secrets."

"No, but they weren't intended for an insensitive clod like you," she shot back irritably. Those letters had been private and personal, filled with homesickness and the yearnings of a young girl trying to find herself. "That's not important now," she said, refusing to be side-tracked. "So, what about my offer?"

"What about mine?" he countered.

"I'm not going to sell this farm, and if I were, you would be the very last person in the universe to get it." The anger she'd been holding in check since the lawyer's appointment stirred around inside her, rising to the surface like oil on water. "Damn it, Judd, there is nothing holding you here, no family, no ties. You're a good worker, I'm sure you could find a job on half a dozen places around the area. This is my home, my roots are buried here. My parents and my grandparents are buried in the little cemetery. This is my farm now and I don't want you here." Her eyes flashed with open hostility.

"It looks like in this particular case you aren't going to get what you want. I'm staying." There was a flat finality in his voice.

"I'm really not surprised," Ginger said, her cool tones hiding her tumultuous emotions. "You've landed yourself a lifetime of job security and a big fat paycheck every month and all you had to do was be nice to an old man for a couple of years."

His smile faded and his voice became ominously soft. "Tread easy, Paprika. You're on thin ice."

She continued in reckless abandon. "You must be dreadfully disappointed that Grandpa didn't leave you the whole farm. Especially after you went to so much trouble." She knew she should stop, she could see the tension that stiffened his body, recognized the glint of danger that darkened his eyes to the color of the sky in an approaching storm. Yes, she knew she should stop, but she couldn't. For too long, she'd harbored a grudge against the tall, attractive man in front of her, and the words shot out of her like jabs from a prize-fighter. "You wormed your way into Grandfather's affections, but there was still the little problem of me."

"Ginger..." He took a threatening step toward her, but she stood her ground, refusing to be daunted.

"How convenient it was for you that I decided to do something stupid and leave here, giving you all the time you needed to wheedle your way into Grandpa's will. What I can't understand is why six years wasn't long enough for you to convince Grandpa to leave everything to you."

In two swift movements, Judd reached out and picked her up, then threw her over his shoulder.

"Put me down," she yelled angrily, flailing her fists against the broadness of his back. Not only was she angry and humiliated, but she was suddenly very much aware of his sun-warmed skin against hers, his intox-icating scent of sweat-tanged maleness. This only served to fuel the fires of her anger even more. "Damn you, Judd Bishop, put me down."

"You came down here spoiling for a fight, making all kinds of hotheaded accusations. I think what you need is to cool off."

Before Ginger realized his intentions, he uncere-moniously dropped her into the water-filled cattle trough.

Ginger's cry of rage became a spewing of water as she surfaced. "How dare you," she gasped, finding her footing and standing up, blinded by hair and water. She swiped her wet hair off her forehead, his amused eyes and laughing lips coming into focus. She hit the water with the flat of her hand, attempting to direct the splash to where he stood. He easily side-stepped out of the way.

"Get me out of here," she said between clenched teeth.

"I'm not coming anywhere near you," he laughed, his eyes lit appreciatively.

Ginger followed his gaze, looking down at herself and gasping in renewed rage and a wealth of embarrassment. Her T-shirt clung to her, transparent and exposing the outline of her delicate, lace-trimmed bra. She tried to splash him again. "Stop gawking and get me out of here."

"Six years in the city may have improved your appearance, but it certainly didn't improve your nature. You're still the most prickly, hotheaded hellion I've ever known." He reached down and grabbed his shirt from the ground, then turned and walked away.

"And you're still the most hardheaded, obnoxious bully I've ever known," she yelled after him. "You just wait, Judd Bishop. I've officially declared war on you."

He didn't turn around, didn't even acknowledge her words of challenge. If he knew Ginger Taylor, he was in for a wicked battle of wills. But it was one he wouldn't lose. Serenity had become as much his home as hers, and he wasn't about to walk away simply because she was acting like a spoiled brat. The thought of a battle with her didn't daunt him—rather, he felt stimulated at the prospect. He'd been challenged by Ginger since the first day he'd arrived at the farm. She'd declared open warfare on him then as well. The result had been molasses in his chest of drawers, shoes nailed to the floor, his bed short sheeted night after night…she'd been a fourteen-year-old guerilla fighter with raging hormones and a predisposition to despise anyone who took her grandfather's attention away from her. She'd been like a young puppy dog, nipping at his heels, never hard enough to do any real damage, but enough to be considered sometimes amusing, occasionally an irritant.

He walked into the back door of the house and pulled a pitcher of water out of the refrigerator. He poured himself a tall glass and sat down at the kitchen table, absently running his hand over the scarred wooden tabletop.

He'd noticed the subtle changes happening before his very eyes before she had left Serenity. He'd seen the signs of approaching womanhood, noticed that she was changing from a girl with tangled hair and knobby knees to a woman with hair the color of passion and skin that always looked dewy and soft. Yes, he'd noticed, and he'd been relieved when she had left.

If the apple was removed from the garden, then there was no temptation. And there had been times when he had looked at Ginger, seen the woman she was becoming, and he had been tempted. He'd wanted to see her unusual cinnamon-colored eyes widen in pleasure as he taught her the ways of desire. Yet, in his desire had been shame. Judd loved and respected Tom Taylor like no man he'd ever known. Tom had given him hope when he'd had none. Tom had validated Judd as a worthwhile human being at a time when Judd had been an angry child wanting only to hurt as he himself had been hurt. It seemed so disrespectful, so ugly that Judd would feel temptation for Tom's granddaughter. It still made him burn with shame.

He now took several long swallows of the water, the ice-cold liquid causing a quick stab of pain over his left eye as he drank it too fast.

He'd thought six years would have transformed any lust he felt for her into indifference, but it hadn't. The minute he'd seen her walking toward him out there in the field, those long legs of hers extending neatly from the minute shorts she wore, he'd felt a lick of lust stroke his insides. And when he'd picked her up and thrown her over his shoulder, the feel of her firm breasts pressed against his back, the curve of her derriere only inches from his face had made heat gather in the pit of his stomach. Finally, when she'd risen up from the cattle trough, in the moments before he'd turned to walk away, he'd seen how her wet clothes molded to her curves, and the heat that had been centered in the pit of his stomach pumped wildly through his veins.

He took his cold water glass and rolled it across his brow. It was crazy. He didn't even like her very much. She was hotheaded and spoiled, ill-tempered and undisciplined. She was also beautiful and spirited and ripe for picking . . . too ripe for comfort.

Well, there was only one thing to do. He was going to have to follow through on his promise to Tom and find Ginger a good husband . . . the quicker the better.

He pulled a sheet of paper from his shirt pocket and spread it out before him on the table. The name Linden Hammonds was at the top, a pencil line carefully drawn through it.

He got up and grabbed a pencil from the cabinet, then returned to the table, his brow wrinkled in thought. Jordon Phillips—he was about the right age for Ginger. Jordon had a decent job running the used-car lot in town. Of course, the man wore plaid suits and colored socks, but Judd had never held the way a man dressed against him. Still, hadn't there been some rumors about Jordon being involved in some shady business deals? And hadn't the Internal Revenue been asking questions? No, he would never do. With a heavy sigh, Judd carefully crossed through *Jordon Phillip*.

Ginger dressed carefully for dinner, choosing the outfit her Aunt Loretta had bought her for her last birthday. Although the rust-colored sheath was dressy for supper at the farm, the classic lines and delicate material made her feel chic and sophisticated. And for some reason she felt she needed a veneer of sophistication to get through the meal.

All afternoon she'd indulged herself in fantasies of revenge against Judd for his humiliating treatment of her earlier in the day. They had been wonderfully wicked fantasies, each one involving various degrees of torture and humiliation for him, the end result each time being his promise to leave the farm forever. But they were just wistful imaginings. Reality was that she had to go downstairs and sit across from him at the table. Thank goodness Ray and Lisa would also be there.

With a last look in her dresser mirror, Ginger left her room and carefully descended the wide staircase. She'd never done well in high heels, preferring her bare feet or thongs. She stifled the impulse to kick them off and breathed a sigh of relief as she safely hit the hall floor at the foot of the stairs. She entered the living room, immediately assailed by a wave of nostalgia as she realized the room was exactly as it had been through her years of growing up. Nothing had changed in the years she had been away. No, that wasn't exactly true, there was one thing missing...the scent of her grandfather's cherry pipe tobacco. The absence of the familiar scent only drove home to her the fact that her grandfather was gone forever.

She moved across the room toward the sofa, stumbling as her heel caught on the edge of the area rug.

"I'm surprised those shoes don't give you altitude nosebleeds."

She whirled around and spied him sitting on one of the bar stools at the portable bar that stood in the corner of the room.

"And I'd think your pride wouldn't allow you to remain where you aren't wanted," she returned with the cool hauteur she'd perfected while in New York.

He chuckled softly. "I've learned over the years that it's not worth maintaining pride if it's at the expense of something I want very badly."

"You'll never get this farm. I'll die before I allow you to own this place."

"Such dramatics. You didn't do any theater work while you were in New York, did you?"

"You are insufferable," she returned, stalking over to the bar, deciding she needed more than determination to get through the evening. She needed a drink.

"There's ice in the bucket," he said as she grabbed a glass. "If you can't find the ice pick, you can always use that sharp tongue of yours."

She ignored his jibe, fixed herself a scotch on the rocks, then eyed him coolly. "So, tell me. What's it going to take to make you leave?"

Judd sighed and with a deft movement of his wrist made the ice swirl around in the bottom of his glass. "You are being redundant, Ginger."

"You're going to find that I'm quite a bore when it comes to this particular topic."

"Does this mean I should be on the alert for salt in my coffee and toads in my bed?" His gray eyes twin-

kled with amusement as he remembered the ways she'd
tormented him when she was younger.

"I think I've graduated from those kinds of childish tricks," she returned. "I'll think of more adult
ways to torment you out of my life."

His dark eyebrows quirked upward and a wicked
smile hovered on his lips. "Sounds utterly fascinating. I can't wait."

She raised her glass in a toast and he did the same.
The clinking of their crystal spoke of the challenge
that sparked in their eyes. "May the best man win,"
she stated crisply, jaunty with the warm scotch in her
belly and confident she would win this battle of wills.

"And to the victor goes the spoils," he added, his
voice a silken caress on her nervous system that made
the scotch she'd just drunk explode and invade her
entire body. As his gaze swept over her, she felt a curious weakening of her knees and the confidence she'd
felt only seconds before wavered, making her wonder
if she was playing a game nobody could win.

Surprisingly, dinner was a pleasant affair. It was as
if Judd and Ginger had nonverbally declared a truce
for the duration of the meal. Lisa served up a steady
stream of chatter along with fried chicken, mashed
potatoes, home-style gravy, and a bevy of vegetables
fresh from the garden.

Lisa's conversation was an amusing blend of gossip
and news, keeping them all entertained and the mood
of the meal light.

"You know the Walkers?" Lisa asked, passing the gravy boat to Ginger, who nodded. "They're selling their place and moving to California."

"Why?" Ginger asked. The Walkers had owned a small farm down the road from Serenity for as long as she could remember.

Lisa shrugged. "They say they're tired of the struggle. Farming isn't as profitable as it used to be and the Walkers have had a couple of really bad years."

"That reminds me, the coops should be ready by next week," Ray said to Judd.

"Coops? What coops?" Ginger looked from Judd to Ray, then back again.

"Chicken coops," Judd said succinctly, as if that explained everything.

Ginger looked at him blankly. "Chicken coops?" she echoed.

"Yes, you know. Those big, long shed like buildings where chickens like to nest."

"I know that," Ginger snapped impatiently. "But since when do we have chickens?"

"Since next week. I've got a brood of two hundred chicks being delivered," Judd explained.

"But why?" she asked with confusion. "Serenity isn't a poultry farm."

"We're diversifying."

Irritation immediately swept over her at the authoritative ring of his voice. He spoke as if the decision had already been made and she had no say in the matter at all. She eyed him defiantly. "I think you've forgotten who is now making the decisions around here." She looked over at Ray. "Ray, what's this about chickens?"

Ray finished chewing a bite of corn, washing it down with a gulp of water, looking first at Judd, then at Ginger in obvious discomfort. "It was Judd's idea. He bounced it off your grandpa and me a couple of months ago. We've got the brooder house already built, and we just need to finish up the last of the three coops." He grimaced. "I thought you already knew about them."

"No, I didn't." She smiled at Ray, then cast Judd an arch look. "But I'm sure Judd is going to tell me all about them."

"Why, I'd be delighted," he returned with mocking servility. "I was reading an article a couple months ago, one of those cautionary cancer stories. It said that consumers should be leery of where they buy their poultry." As he warmed to his subject, his voice lost all traces of condescension, becoming warm and mellow.

Judd continued talking about consumers who were tired of chicken being shot full of growth hormones and special enzymes, and Ginger couldn't help but notice how attractive he was. He wore a white shirt unbuttoned at his throat, exposing bronzed skin. The whiteness of the shirt emphasized the dark of his hair and the clear gray of his eyes. She'd noticed before he sat down that his jeans hugged his slender hips and long legs as if tailored to perfection by a fashion designer. Had he always been so attractive? Yes, even at fourteen years old, she'd been aware of his sexual appeal, but hadn't realized what to call it. There was something in him of a cowboy minus the hat and boots, a touch of the pirate without an eyepatch.

He would be a good lover. She knew this despite her own lack of expertise in that area. He wouldn't be satisfied merely to make love, he'd want to possess a woman, own her, mark her indelibly forever by the experience.

"Honey, are you all right?"

Ginger suddenly became aware of everyone's eyes on her. She realized she'd shredded her napkin into tiny pieces and her thoughts had made her mouth unaccountably dry. "I'm fine," she croaked, grabbing her water glass and taking a sip. She shot an irritable gaze across the table to the man who'd caused her crazy, disconcerting thoughts. "I was just about to nod off to sleep from Judd's technical monologue. All I wanted was a simple explanation as to why we are going into poultry farming."

"Because it's a smart decision," Judd answered darkly.

"Oh, it's a smart decision because it's yours?"

"Actually, it was your grandfather's. He mentioned it to me, and I just sort of expanded on his idea."

Ginger looked at Ray for confirmation, who nodded. Chickens—*gawd,* she hated chickens. "Tomorrow I'd like you to sit down with me and tell me about any other decisions my grandfather made that will change the future of Serenity," she said to Judd. She felt as if things were spinning out of control. The interloper was in charge, making changes that affected the farm, and she felt like a bystander. She didn't like the feeling. She needed to establish her position. "Why don't you meet with me in the morning at nine o'clock in the den? We can sit down and go over everything then."

"Can't. We're starting on the wheat tomorrow. I've got two extra men coming with combines at dawn."

"Then we'll meet just before dawn," she returned evenly, refusing to be put off.

"Fine." His eyes once again lit to a dove gray as amusement lifted one corner of his mouth. "I seem to recall you were always quite a delight in the morning. Sort of like a cross between a grizzly bear and a turtle—either growling at everything that moved or hiding your head."

"I assure you I intend to be most alert when we discuss the future of Serenity," she said coolly. There was nothing worse than having a man note your weaknesses, and mornings had always been a weakness of hers.

"Shall we say around four-thirty?"

"Fine," she answered, stifling a groan at thoughts of rising at that ungodly hour.

"Ginger, you should see the strawberries in the strawberry patch," Lisa said with the fine art of an expert mediator steering the conversation to a neutral topic. "They're as big as your fist and sweet as can be." From here the conversation revolved around the farm, the garden and the orchard.

It was dusk by the time Lisa and Ginger had cleaned up the dishes. As Ginger walked Lisa and Ray out onto the porch, the cicadas had begun their noisy hum, and the air was perfumed with the sweet scent of flowers.

"See you in the morning," Lisa yelled as she and Ray walked across the yard to their car.

Ginger nodded and waved, noticing how Ray patted Lisa's bulging tummy before Lisa got into the car. The gesture, so simple yet implying such intimacy, made a strange longing unfurl inside her.

Other than her grandparents, Ginger had been alone most of her life. And for her childhood years, her grandfather's companionship had been enough. But while in New York, she had gone from child to woman, and she now felt the deep yearnings for a special man in her life.

The strange feeling dissipated as she thought of the man who, at present, was not only the most immediate man around, but the proverbial thorn in her side as well. She couldn't think of another man in her life until she got rid of the one she had. With a deep sigh she turned and went back into the house.

Chapter Three

Judd paced the confines of the small den, aggravation pulling his features into a deep scowl. He looked at his wristwatch for the third time in as many minutes. Where the devil was that infernal woman?

He'd gone by her bedroom door on his way down from his own third-floor quarters nearly half an hour before. He'd heard the sound of a radio playing softly from within and had assumed she was up and getting ready for their predawn meeting. But now he was beginning to wonder. He'd come to the den at precisely four thirty, in accordance with her command the night before. Her command...his lips curved upward as he remembered how hard she had tried to be autocratic. Her attempt had been lost on him. He had too many memories of her that were incongruent with the cool, haughty image she'd tried to present the night before. Damn it, where was she? If she was going to play the queen, issuing orders, the least she could do was be on time.

The longer he waited, the more angry he was becoming. He was a busy man. The weather forecast was calling for unstable weather conditions toward the end of the week, and he wanted to get all the wheat harvested before then. He didn't have the time or the patience to play power games with Ginger.

He strode purposely up the flight of stairs, pausing outside her bedroom door. He could hear the muted sounds of her radio playing mellow rock. Surely she was awake. He rapped lightly on the door, listening for sounds of movement. There were none. He knocked again, this time louder. When there was still no answer he pushed open the door. The room glowed with the pale illumination of predawn. He spotted her immediately, still asleep, lying flat on her back with only her tousled red curls and her face peeking out from beneath the peach-colored sheet.

He wasn't surprised the music from the alarm hadn't awakened her. Tom had often joked that nothing short of an atomic blast moved his granddaughter out of bed before noon.

A smile pulled his mouth upward as he spied a half a glass of water on her bedside stand. No, he couldn't. She was sleeping so soundly, so peacefully, and it would be cruel to awaken her like that. He moved across the room and picked up the water glass. Cruel, yes, but so appropriate. She deserved a payback for all her years of tormenting him.

Yet, as he stood with the glass of water held high over her head, she stirred and a tender smile swept over her sleeping countenance. All desire to douse her with water left him and instead he set the glass back on her nightstand.

What a lovely young woman she had become while away. Her short haircut flattered her, emphasizing the delicate features of her face, the creamy texture of her skin.

Before he realized what he was doing, he reached out and with his fingertip, traced from the outside of the corner of her eyebrow down her cheek and across her lips. Her skin was warm as a summer night, with the softness of morning dew. Her dreamy smile deepened and a sigh escaped her lips where his fingertip lingered. The sigh stirred fantasies, summoned desire. He wanted to kiss her full, sensual lips. He wanted to crawl beneath the cocoon of covers and make love to her, feel her breathless sighs in the hollow of his neck as he stroked her body with slow, languid caresses. He wanted to tame the shrew.

What was he doing? Fantasizing about Ginger, Tom's granddaughter. He'd made a solemn vow to Tom that he would take care of her, see her married to an honest, loving man. So what was he doing standing here lusting for her? He should take the glass of water from her nightstand and pour it over his own head.

He withdrew his hand from her face and took a step backward, accidentally knocking into the nightstand. Ginger's eyes flew open, dazed bewilderment radiating from their coppery depths. As he watched, the dazed expression receded and fury reigned, turning the copper to fire. "What are you doing in here?" She sat up, holding the sheet in front of her like a shield of armor against a marauding knight.

"Don't worry, your virtue is safe with me," he snapped, irritated by the anger she always aimed at him, even more aggravated by the desire he'd felt for her only moments before.

"And what makes you think I have any virtue left to worry about?" she returned with a flippancy she didn't feel.

She was immediately sorry when his eyes deepened to a slate hue and he moved closer to the bed. His hand reached out and captured one of her fire-kissed curls between his fingers. "Are you telling me you had a lover while you were in New York?"

"I'm not telling you anything. What I did while I was in New York was my business." She jerked her head away from his touch and eyed him boldly. "Besides, what makes you think it was only one lover? I might have had a dozen."

"Oh, I don't think so, Paprika." His lips curved upward and he leaned down so that he was at eye level, his breath a fan of warmth on her face. "No, I don't think there were any lovers in New York." As he said these words he reached up and once again traced the contours of her cheek, allowing the caress to trail from her face to follow the curve of her collarbone and linger in the hollow of her throat.

Ginger's breath caught in her chest, and her stomach tightened in response to his touch. She could feel the warmth of his body so close to hers, and it caused a slumberous weight to steal over her. His thumb was moving back and forth at the base of her throat, hypnotic and entrancing. She tried to answer him but found her mouth unnaturally dry. And she was having trouble remembering what his question had been . . . if there had been a question at all.

"No, I know you haven't known the intimacy of making love to a man," he continued, his voice low and throaty. "I can see it in your eyes. I can feel your innocence here." He laid his hand against her heart, which was beating like that of a captured, frightened bird. He jerked his hand away and stood up. "Besides," he continued, "no man in his right mind would chance making love with you unless he wouldn't mind sporting the wounds of a she-devil in heat."

The languid weight that had held her motionless snapped like a brittle branch in the middle of a wind storm. "Well, you don't have to worry about whether I scratch my mate or not, because you'll never get the opportunity to find out."

"When I take a woman in my arms, I want to feel softness and acquiescence, not thistles and thorns."

"Get out of here," Ginger yelled, reaching out to grab something, anything she could throw at him. Her hand closed around the water glass on her nightstand and she grabbed it up, unaware of the liquid it contained until the water splashed onto the front of her nightgown. She squealed in surprise and outrage as the sound of his mocking laughter filled the room.

"I just can't understand why it is that lately every time I see you I'm reminded of a mad, wet hen." He moved to the door.

His words made her remember his undignified treatment of her the day before at the cattle trough. With an explosive yowl, she released the glass from her hand.

In the blink of an eye he was out of the door, closing it just as the glass careered into it with a dull thud.

Judd stalked down the stairs, letting his anger build. The anger felt good. It was such a clean and uncomplicated emotion compared to the others he'd felt only moments before.

Desire . . . how could he feel so much desire for a hellcat like Ginger? How could he crave something he didn't even like? He didn't like spinach and he sure as hell never got a sudden craving to play Popeye and pop open a can.

He stepped outside onto the porch, taking a deep breath of the morning-scented air. The men would be arriving soon, as the horizon was painted in pinks and golds, announcing the imminent arrival of dawn.

He sat down on the old rocking chair where Tom had often sat to watch the day break, Judd's mind still upstairs in Ginger's bedroom. The thought of Ginger making love with some cosmopolitan New Yorker had caused a gut-wrenching reaction in the pit of his stomach. He'd wanted to grab her up in his arms, erase the memory of any past lover, leave a brand that would be seen by any future lover.

He rubbed his hands over his face in bewilderment. What chemistry was at work, what magic had him thinking such crazy thoughts?

He would never want to get tangled up with a woman like Ginger. It would be like the Fourth of July every day, all fireworks and explosions. He was more inclined toward soft-spoken, even-tempered women whose only perfume was the doughy scent of freshly baked bread. If he was going to get involved with a woman, it would be somebody like Amanda Withers, the pert blonde who owned the café in town. He'd dated Amanda off and on for several months and found her agreeable, affectionate and peaceful. Funny, he couldn't remember exactly why he'd stopped seeing her a couple of months before.

He stood up, hearing the distant rumbling of approaching farm equipment. It was going to be a long day, and the last thing he needed was thoughts of a certain red-haired enchantress whose body promised heavenly delights and whose scathing temper, the heat of hell's fires.

Ginger reached up and, with her toe, manipulated the hot water faucet off, not wanting to move any other portion of her body out of the hot water and

scented bubbles that surrounded her. She could remember her grandmother telling her once that no
problem was so big that it couldn't be solved by a long
soak in a hot tub. Ginger figured she'd have to soak at
least a week to even begin to figure out the chaos that
was in her brain.

She'd been sleeping so peacefully, dreaming of a
man who was running his hand down the side of her
face, touching her with the infinite tenderness of a
man in love. Then, to awaken and look into those
hateful gray eyes, the infuriatingly handsome face of
her nemesis.

"He's lucky I didn't strangle him," she muttered,
reaching for the soap.

As she worked the bar of soap into a thick lather
across her shoulders, her mind replayed what had
happened in her bedroom.

She didn't know what had possessed her to inti-
mate to him that she'd had lovers in New York. It certainly wasn't true. Oh, she'd had many dates. Her
Aunt Loretta had done her best to play matchmaker
for Ginger. There had been dates with attractive men,
most of them financially secure and all of them nice.
But none of them had been able to touch the secret
core of Ginger's heart. She had not felt the heady ex-
hilaration of physical temptation, not until moments
before when Judd had blazed a trail of teasing exploration with his work-roughened fingertip. His touch
had evoked feelings that were alien; frightening yet
intoxicating as a glass of burgundy brew.

She slid deeper into the water, finding no solace in the liquid warmth. If anything, it only served to remind her of the pervasive warmth of his body so close to hers on the bed.

With a groan of disgust Ginger submerged herself completely, wondering if the water was boiling from the steam of her inner thoughts.

Moments later as she dried off and got dressed, she thought about his words just before he had left her room. He'd said something about wanting softness and acquiescence in his woman. Fine, let him go find some mealy-mouthed, Milquetoast kind of woman to seduce and caress.

She must never forget that because of Judd, she'd lost six years of sharing her grandfather's life. She must never forget that Judd was a trespasser who'd gained a foothold here on the farm because of the weakness of another. Most of all, she must never let go of the fact that Judd had denied her the chance to be a part of the end of her grandfather's life.

Strange and frightening emotions firmly under control, Ginger went downstairs to find Lisa just coming in the back door.

"My, my, up before the chickens," Lisa said, going directly to the coffee pot and the canister of coffee.

"Don't say anything about chickens," Ginger replied, sliding into a chair at the table.

"Oh, that's right. You were going to meet with Judd this morning. How did it go?" She finished pouring the water into the coffee machine.

"It didn't go. I overslept," Ginger admitted.

"Whew, I'll bet Judd was mad. One of his biggest pet peeves is to be kept waiting."

"Oh, really?" Ginger filed this bit of information away to be used at another time. "What are some of his other pet peeves?" she asked innocently.

"Oh, he hates it when..." Lisa laughed. "Oh no, I see that devilish light in your eyes. You aren't about to get me involved in your war with Judd." Lisa's expression turned serious. "I love you both."

"How can you love a cold, arrogant man like Judd Bishop?"

"The same way I grew to love the stoic, silent man I'm married to." She smiled at Ginger's look of confusion. "Honey, sometimes you have to look beneath the outward appearances. If you dig beneath the layers, you might be surprised at what you find."

"I know what I'd find—a black heart to match his soul," Ginger replied dryly. "Anyway, I don't want to talk about him. I thought I'd drive into town this morning and pick up a few things, stop in and say hello to a few people."

"Be sure and stop in at May's Groceries. May asks about you all the time."

Ginger nodded, thanking Lisa as she poured them each a cup of coffee and joined Ginger at the table. "Is there anything you want me to pick up for you while I'm out?"

Lisa shook her head. "I can't think of anything. Judd usually buys any groceries I need."

"From now on I'll get what you need. Judd is going to be much too busy now to take care of buying supplies. I'm going to buy house paint today. I can't believe how he's let things go around here."

"Judd had his hands pretty full with your grandfather's ideas about the chickens."

"Yes, I'm sure it took hours upon hours to convince Grandpa to add the codicil to the will that assured him a place here forever."

Lisa opened her mouth to protest or defend, then shut it abruptly. She eyed Ginger with a small smile. "I'm not going to try to change your mind about Judd. I know you wouldn't listen anyway. When you were younger you always got yourself into trouble because you led with your emotions and not your brains. You judged and sentenced Judd based on the perceptions of a fourteen-year-old. Don't you think it's time you learned to know him as a woman, without those youthful impressions?"

"It's obvious Judd has been successful in pulling the wool over your eyes as well as Grandfather's. I'm not so gullible, and no, I don't intend to give him a chance to prove how wonderful he is. He stole Grandpa from me. He didn't even give me a chance to help make the final arrangements for the funeral." Ginger's voice caught in her throat.

"Oh, honey." Lisa tried to embrace her, but Ginger waved her away.

"Don't worry, I'm not going to break down and cry." She sniffed and offered Lisa a tremulous smile.

"You know what Grandpa always said, 'If you're going to cry, do it over a flower. No sense wasting all that moisture.'"

Lisa laughed. "Yes, your grandpa was quite a man... the last of the true pioneers."

For a moment the two women sipped their coffee, each of them entertaining their own special memories of Tom Taylor.

"Where are those chicken coops Ray and Judd were talking about last night?" Ginger asked. "I walked down to the pasture yesterday, but I didn't see anything."

"They're out back, beyond the garden and over the ridge."

"I think I'll go have a look before I head into town." Ginger finished her coffee and stood up. "I should be back before noon."

The garden had always been Tom's pride and joy. The fifty-by-a-hundred-foot plot was lush with vegetables. Lettuce, tomatoes, green beans, new potatoes—Tom had babied them all. He'd often said that the ground was so fertile if he planted Ginger's toes, he'd probably grow ten new Gingers.

Her smile at the memory lingered for a moment, then faded as she caught sight of the small, barren plot of dirt next to the big garden. This had been her garden. Every spring, while her grandpa had seeded his big one, Ginger had tended to her own little area. In the evenings they'd worked together to weed and water, issuing challenges on whose would see the first outward sign of life, the first sprout pushing aside the dirt to reach for the sunlight. But now, her garden lay brown and bare and she wondered if her grandpa had thought of her every time he'd come out here to work on his.

Biting her bottom lip, she walked past the gardens and crested the ridge. There, in a huge fenced area, she saw the three coops. Ray was working on one of them, hammering the boards along one side. He raised a hand in greeting as she approached.

"So, these are the coops," she said, stepping through the opening of the chicken-wire fence.

"Yup." Ray put his hammer down and swiped his sweaty brow with the back of one arm.

"I can't believe we're doing this. I don't know anything about chickens, do you?"

"Nope, but I guess we'll learn."

"Why does this one look different?" Ginger walked to the last of the coops, which was smaller than the other two.

"That's the brooder house. That's where the chicks are kept until they're fully feathered, then they go to the other coops."

Ginger nodded. Gawd, she hated chickens, with their beady eyes and scratching, pecking natures. If they had to diversify, why couldn't they do it with cuddly sheep, or additional cattle? Of all the animals in the animal kingdom, why had Judd decided to go with chickens? As far as she was concerned, it was just another black mark against him.

"I'm driving into town, anything you need?"

Ray shook his head and with a wave of her hand, Ginger headed back to the house and her car.

It was only a fifteen-minute drive to the town of Gentry, Kansas. As always on a warm, early-summer day, the town appeared almost deserted. But Ginger knew that on a rainy morning, the town came alive as the fields became too wet to work in and time lay heavy on farmers' hands. On those days the parking spaces in front of the Great Day Café were filled with pickup trucks.

This morning Ginger was able to choose her own parking space from the empty row, so she parked right in front of the hardware store where she would be making most of her purchases.

It took her almost half an hour to pick out the paint she wanted for the house and load the gallon cans into her trunk. On impulse, she also bought a door lock. Never again would Judd Bishop sneak into her bedroom without her being aware of him.

After the hardware store, she walked across the street to May's Groceries.

"Hi, Ginger." The wizened old woman behind the cash register greeted her as if it had been only a day instead of six years since Ginger had last been in the store.

"Hi, May. How are you?"

"Still breathing, so I can't complain." May grabbed a huge glass container of licorice twists and held it out to Ginger.

"Thanks." Ginger reached in and pulled one out. It was an age-old ritual. Every time Tom had come to town, he'd brought Ginger, and while he shopped, Ginger had sat with May, discussing the problems of the world and gorging herself on licorice twists.

"I knew you'd be coming home. Your grandpa told me. Last night in a dream he came to me and told me his Ginger was coming home to take care of things."

Ginger smiled, long ago accustomed to the eccentricities of the old woman. It had been May who had introduced Ginger to the ideas of time travel, UFOs and ESP. "Yes, I'm home now and I'm going to take care of things."

May nodded in satisfaction. "It's only right that a Taylor should be in charge of Serenity, not some stranger who showed up out of nowhere."

"My sentiments exactly," Ginger agreed, pleased to find somebody else who was in accordance with her about Judd. It didn't matter that May also believed she'd been abducted by a UFO for a week, or that she thought herself to be the reincarnation of Mary, Queen of Scots. It was enough that May also believed there was no place for Judd at Serenity.

"The big city wasn't to your liking." It was more a statement than a question. "You're a Taylor, Ginger, and you belong here on the land, just like your grandpa and his pa before him."

"Well, I'm home now, and I'm home to stay."

It was nearing noon when Ginger pulled back up the driveway to the farm. She'd enjoyed visiting in town, but remembered she'd told Lisa she'd be home before noon.

"Where's everyone else?" she asked when Lisa called her for lunch and she saw the table was set for just the two of them.

"Oh, Judd and Ray never eat lunch when they're harvesting. One of them will come in later this afternoon for sandwiches to be taken out to the field. Then they'll work until dusk."

Ginger and Lisa indulged themselves in women talk for the duration of the meal, then Ginger went upstairs to set to work placing the lock on her bedroom door. She had just finished installing it when she heard heavy footsteps climbing the stairs. She turned to see Judd coming down the hallway. As he spied her, his steps slowed and that mocking grin swept over his face, making her nerves jump to the surface of her skin.

"Doing a little maintenance, are you?" he asked, eyeing the screwdriver and hammer she held in her hands.

"Installing a lock," she answered coolly. She wished he would step back. He was standing so close to her she could smell the tang of his male sweat, the earthy scent of ripened wheat and the freshness of sunshine.

"Are you hoping to lock somebody out, or keep somebody in?"

"Lock you out," she answered irritably. "You seem to lack respect for my privacy."

"And you think this flimsy piece of metal will keep me out if I want to come in?" There was a challenging flinty steel in his eyes. "Get in the room and lock the door." He gave her a gentle push into the bedroom.

Ginger closed the door and threw the lock, then stood back, her heart thudding rapidly in her chest. He's going to try to break down the door, and it's just a game, she told herself. Yet she felt as if they had transcended games, that the challenge she'd seen in his eyes had nothing to do with the lock on the door. If she was lucky, he'd use his head as a battering ram and find the lock an immovable object. At the same instant this pleasant thought crossed her mind, he hit the door with a loud crash and it flew open, the lock hanging broken on the jamb. For a moment they stared at each other, then in three quick strides he reached her. His hard face was inches from hers, so close she could see the rough texture of his skin, the shadowed darkness of his whiskers.

He's going to kiss me, she thought. His mouth took hers in explosive demand and all other thoughts fled from her mind. Nothing in her experience had prepared her for the fire and ice of his kiss. Nothing in her past had prepared her for the desire that streaked through her like lightning across a stormy sky.

As quickly as he'd claimed her, he let her go, stepping back from her, the easy amusement back in his eyes. "You see, Paprika, if I wanted you, nothing could keep me out. I guess you're just lucky that I don't want you.'' He turned and left the room.

Ginger sat down on the bed, fearing her shaking legs would hold her up no longer. She ran a finger across her lips, realizing her bottom one was swollen and her chin felt raw from the contact with his unshaven skin. His words should have infuriated her, but they didn't. She'd felt his heart beating as rapidly as her own while he kissed her.

She'd tasted the desire on his lips, seen it burning in his eyes. His words said one thing, but his body had betrayed him. He wanted her, and in that she had her weapon to use to get him to leave Serenity forever.

Chapter Four

He wanted her. It was a surge of power that sang in her veins. He desired her. The knowledge was like the refrain of her favorite song spinning around and around in her head.

Yet it was impossible to put this new knowledge to use, because for the next four days she didn't see him. He was gone in the mornings before she got up and didn't return until after dusk, when he showered and shaved, then left again not to return until late in the night.

Still she was having fun playing subtle little games calculated to crawl under his skin. She spritzed her perfume liberally in the bathroom they shared so her scent would linger there no matter when he went in. She left a pair of black hose hanging from the shower rod, a sexy nightgown on the hook behind the door. It was an age-old game she played, using the weapon women had used since the beginning of time.

She also spent the four days at the kitchen table, with the farm books spread out before her. Mr. Roberts had led her to believe that she was financially comfortable, but as she went over the books she realized it was a comfort built on unstable ground. A season of bad weather, falling grain prices...her finances were contingent on so many uncontrollable factors. The price of beef was down, poultry was up. As much as she hated to admit it, Judd seemed to have a sound idea with the chickens. Thank goodness he should be finished with the wheat today. The weatherman was calling for evening storms, and a hard rain could be as damaging to ripe wheat as a moth to a sweater.

She closed the books in front of her, stood up and stretched, arms overhead. She moved to the window, looking out to the distant field where she could see the combine making wide swathes through the golden grain. She could easily envision Judd on the seat, his gray eyes proprietary as he surveyed the land. He would sit on the combine with the confidence and ease of a cowboy sitting on his favorite horse, his strong, bronzed arms easily controlling the horsepower of the machine.

She turned away from the window, disgruntled that all her efforts to make him leave had, thus far, been fruitless. For a moment she considered reverting to her old childish tricks, but the minute the idea entered her brain, she dismissed it. It hadn't worked years before and she knew it wouldn't work now. Besides, she was no longer a child, and it was time to put childish games behind her.

She plucked peevishly at her blouse, which was sticking to her uncomfortably. She moved back over to the window, this time looking toward the southwest, where the sky had begun to darken ominously. She didn't need to see the approaching black clouds to know it was going to storm. She could feel it in the sticky humidity, in the heavy stillness of the air. She hated storms, had always had an irrational fear of the crashing thunder and the flashing lightning. It was a childhood fear she'd carried with her into adulthood, like a piece of unwanted luggage.

She turned away from the window once again, not wanting to allow her gaze to seek out once more the combine and the man who was driving it.

I'll take a bath, she decided. Get rid of the sticky clothes and put on a nice, cool sundress.

As she waited for the water to fill in the tub, she thought about the meeting she'd set up with Judd for that evening. She had finally pinned him down that morning and insisted he meet with her after dinner.

She got into the tub, her mind organizing all the things she wanted to discuss with him. She wanted to find out about the chickens that were going to be delivered day after tomorrow. If she was going to own a chicken farm, then she wanted to learn about them. She also wanted to get him started on painting the house. Every time she went outside and saw the sad, neglectful appearance she got angry with him all over again. What had he been doing these past months?

She laid her head back against the cool porcelain behind her, feeling her body responding to the relaxing warmth of the water. She was tired. For the past three nights she hadn't been able to drop off to sleep until she'd heard Judd's heavy footsteps in the hallway passing her bedroom door. Only when she'd known he was home had she been able to drift off into a dreamless sleep. She now closed her eyes and allowed her muscles to relax completely.

Judd shut down the combine and wiped his sweaty forehead with the back of his hand. Done... and just in the nick of time by the look of the dark clouds rolling in from the south. It would still be a couple of hours before the storm was right on top of them, but he was glad the wheat was in.

He looked around, surveying the now bare field. God, how he wished Tom were here to share this moment of accomplishment. How he missed the old man's sage advice, his companionship. He could imagine Tom sitting next to him now, his aged and weather-worn face creased into an expression of pleasure. "You done good, boy." Those four words, uttered with a twinkling of his eyes, were as close to praise as Tom ever came. Yet Judd felt warmed and proud whenever Tom had said them to him.

"Oh, Tom, why did you leave me such an impossible task?" he now said, crawling down from the combine and stretching his stiff muscles.

"Find a good man for my Ginger," Tom had pleaded, his eyes burning with urgency in his thin, pale face.

Judd hadn't been able to deny the man this last wish. It had nothing to do with the fact that Tom was dying. It had everything to do with love. If Tom had asked him to turn himself inside out, Judd would have done his damnedest to accomplish it.

"Find a good man for Ginger," he scoffed, peeling off the T-shirt that sucked at his skin. Ginger. For the past three days, ever since the foolish impulse that had led him to kiss her, he couldn't get her out of his mind. The scent of her seemed to fill every corner of the house. He'd seen her dark hose and nightgown hanging in the bathroom and had immediately been tortured with visions of what she would look like wearing those things. It was those kinds of visions that had driven him out of the house each night.

He'd spent the last three evenings with Amanda Withers. It had been nice to be in the company of a woman who hung on his every word, agreed with everything he said, looked at him as if he had the answers to every question in the world.

But his evenings with Amanda had not solved his problem of finding a husband for Ginger. So far he had four names on his list of prospects and four names crossed off. Finding a good man for Ginger was like searching for a teardrop in a rainstorm.

He pushed this particular problem out of his mind. At the moment the only thing he wanted was a big glass of water and a hot shower. He headed toward the house, feeling sluggish from the heavy humidity in the air.

In the kitchen he poured himself a large glass of iced water, automatically listening for sounds of Ginger. There were none. She's probably out inspecting the chicken coops, looking for flaws, he thought wryly.

Roger Howell. The name popped into his head as he climbed the stairs toward the bathroom. Roger was just about Ginger's age, and Judd supposed most women would find him attractive, with his clean-cut features and blond hair. Roger worked in the family real estate business and seemed to be doing quite well for himself. Yes, Roger Howell might be just the man Judd was looking for.

As he pushed open the bathroom door, all thoughts of Roger Howell left his mind. In fact, his entire thinking process shut down as he was overwhelmed by the vision before him. She was asleep, her head to one side, her cheek resting against the cool porcelain of the tub, her hair clinging in damp ringlets around her face. Her cheeks were flushed a pale pink from the heat of the water and her long eyelashes were darkened with moisture. Why was it that when she slept she looked so vulnerable, so touchable. Her shoulders were visible above the waterline, gleaming curves of ivory flesh dotted with sun kisses in the shape of freckles. Judd's hands began to tremble as he imagined pressing his lips against each and every one of those cute brown spots.

The bubbles in the water had begun to dissipate, and he could just make out the faint outline of her breasts. He wanted to pick up the bar of soap that rested in the soap dish and run it slowly down the length of her. He wondered if her body had ever been stroked by a lover's touch. When he looked into her eyes, he saw the innocence of a woman unawakened. But looking at her now, he wondered how any man she'd met while in New York had managed to keep his hands off her.

He backed out, quietly shutting the door, realizing his entire body was shaking and a fine sheen of sweat had broken out over his upper lip.

Something has to be done, he thought when he was back downstairs at the kitchen table. *Roger Howell*— he clung to the name like a man hanging on to a lifeboat in a storm-tossed sea.

If he could get Ginger married, fulfill his promise to Tom, then maybe it would be wise for him to consider moving on. Despite the wisdom of this, his heart rebelled at the thought of leaving Serenity. This was his home. His heart, his soul lay in the fields and outbuildings. Every good moment of his life had been spent here, every good memory he possessed had been created here. He was just beginning to realize the farm's potential. Bringing in the chickens was just the first step in a series that would allow Serenity to fulfill the vision he'd had since he was fifteen years old.

The thought of leaving made his heart ache in much the same way he'd hurt when Tom had died.

No, the answer wasn't for him to leave, at least not yet. There were just too many things he wanted to accomplish before he moved on.

In the meantime, he decided a dousing beneath the garden hose might not be such a bad idea. Hopefully it would not only cool off his body, but his overactive imagination as well.

Ginger awoke with a start, discovering her bath water had turned cold and her fingers and toes had become prune clones. She turned on the shower and quickly rinsed off, then dried and wrapped herself in a big towel.

As she walked out into the hallway, she heard the sounds of clattering dishes, the noisy screech of the oven door being opened. Lisa must have arrived while I was in the bathtub, she thought, darting into her bedroom. Minutes later she descended the stairs, dressed in a light cotton sundress.

She stopped in the doorway of the kitchen, surprised to see Judd there, his shirtsleeves rolled up as he stirred something that cooked on the top of the stove.

"Where's Lisa?" she asked, leaning against the door jamb.

"Ray called earlier and said she wasn't feeling well. I told him to keep her in bed and we could fend for ourselves this evening," he replied without looking up from the stove. "I hope you like goulash, and I've got a salad in the refrigerator and garlic bread in the oven.''

"That's fine," she said absently, moving over to the window and staring out. A false twilight had fallen as the storm approached. She shivered and wrapped her arms around herself as she saw the distant lightning, then moments later heard the rumbling of thunder. "I guess the weatherman was right this morning when he predicted rain," she said, turning back around to face him.

"Yeah, we're under a severe thunderstorm watch." He shut off the oven and removed the foil-wrapped loaf of garlic bread.

"Is there anything I can do?" she asked, coming to stand just behind him.

Judd was aware of the scent emanating from her, the same wildflower fragrance that had seemed to be everywhere he went the past couple of days. From the corner of his eye he caught a glimpse of the feminine, pale blue sundress that bared her shoulders…the same shoulders he'd seen earlier while she was in the bath. "You can sit down and get out of my way," he said gruffly, not wanting to be reminded of the vision of her in the tub.

"Well, excuse me," she snapped, stamping over to the table and sitting down.

This is safer, he thought, feeling her hostility rolling off her in waves. There was something comfortable in placing her back in the position of adversary. He spooned the goulash into a serving dish, placed the bread on the table, then grabbed the salad from the refrigerator.

He joined her at the table, aware of her copper gaze on him, aware that she was angry with him for the way he had snapped at her moments before. That was one thing he'd always admired about Ginger. She never tried to hide her emotions. If she didn't like you, you were the first to know it. And she made it quite clear that she didn't like him. That was fine. He'd always thought she was spoiled, indulged by her grandfather, impulsive to a fault.

The only things he and Ginger had in common were the love of her grandfather and the love of this land. And these were the things that would bind them together for years to come, no matter how they felt about each other.

"Did you get all the wheat in?" she asked, her voice cool as she reached to take a piece of the warm garlic bread.

He nodded. "Ray's taking the last truckload to the grain elevator tomorrow."

"Good, then you'll be free to begin painting in the morning."

He stared at her blankly. "Painting what?"

"The house. In case you haven't noticed, you've allowed everything to go to hell around here." Accusation lit her eyes as she glared at him.

"I've allowed?" He kept his tone deceptively soft. "While you were away in New York playing debutante and going to that fancy fashion school, I was busting my butt around here to make sure the profit margins could keep you in designer clothes.''

''That's a low blow,'' she hissed. ''You know I never cared anything about designer clothes, and I had intended to get a degree from that 'fancy school.'''

''You sure didn't hesitate to leave here and break your grandfather's heart,'' he returned.

She gasped in shock, her face draining of all color. The guilt his words evoked made her almost physically ill. She pushed away from the table and stood up, her face an unhealthy shade of white. ''I'm really not very hungry,'' she murmured, and before he could protest, she turned and fled the room.

''Damn,'' Judd swore, slapping his palm down on the tabletop. Whatever had possessed him to say that, to intentionally inflict hurt? To a certain extent it wasn't even true. Sure, initially Tom had been hurt and upset when Ginger had stormed off, but once he knew she had gone to Loretta's, Tom had come to the conclusion that perhaps it was for the best. Ginger needed to get away from Serenity, see what else the world had to offer. And Tom had been pleased that Ginger would be staying at Loretta's, living with the influence of a woman. Tom had always worried that his granddaughter had spent too many of her formative years in the company of men. He'd even been pleased when Ginger had written him and told him of her decision to attend a school of fashion, become a fashion consultant, something she couldn't have done if she'd remained in Gentry.

What Judd simply couldn't understand was why in the hell he felt such a need to drive a wedge between Ginger and himself.

Ginger walked over to her bedroom window, the storm clouds outside reflecting her tumultuous thoughts. Damn him . . . damn Judd Bishop for making her face what had been in her heart since returning to the farm. Guilt—what a heavy burden it was when carried on your shoulders. She would never forgive herself for making a foolish choice years before, and she would never forgive Judd for being the catalyst that had prompted her decision.

It had been easy six years ago to decide to leave Serenity. At the time it had seemed the only thing to do. She'd been driven by feelings of betrayal, isolated from her grandfather by Judd, who'd taken a position between them.

The night she had decided to leave, she'd overheard a conversation between Judd and her grandfather. The two men had been sitting on the porch, as they did every evening after dinner. Ginger had listened to them from the doorway, neither of them knowing she was there. They talked about the crops, laughing about the experiences they'd shared that day. Their conversation seemed like a curious kind of code, marked by comfortable silences, half-finished phrases that spoke of the closeness of the two. After a particularly long silence, Ginger's grandfather had leaned over and touched Judd's shoulder. "I'm glad you're here, Judd. You've filled a void."

Nine little words that had pierced straight through Ginger's heart. Judd had filled whatever void it was her grandfather had. She hadn't been enough, and suddenly her feeling of isolation was devastating. She'd packed her bags that night.

The passing years since then had given her a slightly different perspective. She saw her actions now as those of a child who decided to run away. *They'll miss me when I'm gone, they'll beg me to come back...* It had been those kinds of childish sentiments that had spurred her on.

But Judd's words of moments before had made her realize how thoughtless she'd been. She'd hurt her grandfather, and now there was no way she could ever make it up to him. The penalty for her childishness had been not being here when her grandfather had suffered the heart attack, not being here to tell him goodbye.

She moved away from the window as a bolt of lightning ripped through the sky, causing the hair on the back of her neck to stand out. Almost immediately thunder boomed, making her clap her hands over her ears. Panic welled up in her throat. It was difficult for her to swallow.

This is ridiculous, she thought, pacing the floor, her heart pounding painfully in her chest. I'm an adult, and it's stupid to be afraid of a storm. Still, no matter how she rationalized it, her fear refused to go away. As much as she hated the thought of going back downstairs with Judd, she hated staying up here alone more.

He was just finishing cleaning up the dishes when she reappeared. "I was wondering how long it would take for you to get back down here," he said, putting the last dish in the dishwasher.

She flushed, disliking the fact that he knew her weakness. "Maybe this would be a good time for you to explain exactly what you have in mind for the chickens."

"Okay." He started to pull out a chair at the table.

"Why don't we go into the office," she suggested, thinking of the heavily lined, dark curtains that hung at the windows in that room.

"Okay," he agreed again, a small smile lighting his eyes, letting her know he knew her reason for wanting to go into that particular room.

The minute they stepped into the office, Ginger regretted it. This was the only room she hadn't been in since returning home. She had known that of all the rooms in the house, this one would hold the essence of her grandpa's spirit. From the big oak desk he had bought years before at an auction, to the faint, lingering scent of his pipe, she half expected him to follow them in and ease himself down in the swivel chair behind the desk.

Instead she felt deep resentment sweep over her as Judd sat down in her grandfather's chair.

"Must you sit there?" she snapped.

He studied her for a long moment, then shrugged and moved to one of the two straight-backed chairs that sat in front of the desk.

Ginger walked slowly around the room, her hands moving to touch things she knew had been dear to her grandfather's heart. A built-in bookcase held volumes on farming, framed photographs and memorabilia. A clay ashtray molded in third-grade art class, a flower created out of construction paper, everything she had ever made for him held a place of honor on the shelves. Memories of her grandfather came tumbling back, bringing with it the grief she'd not yet acknowledged.

"Why can't it be that when somebody dies, all memories are wiped away from those who are left behind?" Her voice was full of the tears she'd held in since learning of his death. Until now his passing hadn't seemed real, but now the terrible finality surrounded her.

She sensed Judd getting up and coming to stand behind her. "You miss him." It was a statement of fact uttered softly.

She whirled around to face him, her grief sucking her into a vortex of emotion so intense it frightened her. "Of course I miss him," she exclaimed, grabbing on to the one emotion she recognized—anger. "I loved him, but what would you know about that? You didn't care about him—all you wanted was this farm."

"You spoiled, insensitive brat," Judd said harshly, backing her up against the bookshelf. "Do you think you've cornered the market on grief? On love? Do you honestly believe your grandfather was the kind of man only *you* could love?''

Ginger looked into his eyes; slate orbs that radiated anger. Yet, beneath the anger she saw his grief, deep and profound, and it contradicted everything she'd believed about him. She didn't want to see it, she didn't want to believe that he'd loved her grandfather and was grieving for him. To believe that would make Judd too human,

With a strangled cry, she pushed by him, needing to escape. Without conscious thought she flew out the front door and into the storm, which had unleashed its fury.

Chapter Five

Judd stood for a long moment after she ran out, his anger creating a choking sensation in the back of his throat. Damn her for her conviction that he'd never really cared for her grandfather. And damn his own pride for keeping his love for Tom so closely guarded.

He left the office and went to stand at the living room window, wincing as intense white lightning blinded him for a moment. Why was she so blind? Why couldn't she see that he grieved for Tom as deeply as she? A clap of thunder boomed overhead, rattling the window before him with its intensity.

Where had she gone? His anger dissipated somewhat as nagging worry replaced it. He knew as well as anyone Ginger's fear of storms. He stared out the window, watching the dark silhouette of the trees bend and sway with the blowing of the wind. The rain was coming down in torrents, washing away the last of his anger. Where was Ginger? She shouldn't be out in this mess.

"Serves her right," he muttered, opening the hall closet and pulling out a rain slicker. "Maybe the wind will blow some sense into that brain of hers," he grumbled, irritated because he didn't know which of them was a bigger fool, her for running out in the first place, or him for going out after her. With a colorful curse, he opened the front door and entered the storm.

The rain stung his face as he looked first to the left, then to the right, wondering which way she had gone. To the left was the shed that housed most of the farm machinery, beyond that, the barn. To the right was the old smokehouse, now used for storage. It was there he went, somehow knowing instinctively that's where she would have headed to get out of the storm. Growing up, she had spent many hours playing in the smokehouse amid the cast-off furniture, building forts against imaginary enemies, playing house with her dolls.

The door creaked open as he pushed on it. The interior of the smokehouse was pitch black, but he knew she was there. He could smell her perfume lingering in the air, hear the sounds of her pitiful sobs.

He waited until a flash of lightning lit the sky, then he saw her, curled up on an old sofa that was against one wall. He shrugged off the soaked slicker and laid it on the floor, then approached her as if she were a frightened, wounded animal.

"Ginger, it's all right. Don't be afraid." He kept his voice low, hoping the tones would soothe her fears. "The storm is passing now. It will be gone in a few minutes." He sat down next to her on the sofa and pulled her into his arms.

For a moment she held herself rigidly away from him, but as the storm called out its thunderous roar, she buried her head against his chest, her arms clutching in terror around his neck.

Judd felt a wave of tenderness sweep over him, an emotion strange and alien to his nature. It was so rare for Ginger to show weakness, to allow herself the luxury of tears. She felt so small, so vulnerable in his arms. Her body shook with the power of her sobs, and her tears soaked his shirt. "Shh, it's all right. It will be over soon," he repeated, gently patting her back.

"No...no, it's not all right. It will never be all right again." The words came between hiccuping sobs. She raised up slightly and looked at him, her cinnamon-colored eyes awash with tears. "He's gone, Judd. He's gone forever." She buried her face once again.

Judd's heart ached as he realized her tears were not of fear, but rather tears of grief, long denied, but necessary for healing. He tightened his grip on her, wishing through some sort of emotional osmosis he could take some of her pain away, shoulder it himself. He was long accustomed to dealing with grief.

"Let it all out," he whispered, stroking her fragrant hair softly. He held her tightly, hoping that in his arms she could find comfort. He held her as the sobs subsided, leaving her uttering occasional convulsive gasps. He held her long after the storm had passed. She remained cuddled in his arms long into the night.

"Ginger," Judd yelled, staring at the open paint can before him. "Ginger, I think you've made a mistake."

Ginger came out the back door carrying paintbrushes. "What do you mean I made a mistake?" There was an edge to her voice, one that had been there all morning.

"This paint is blue."

"Yes, it is," she replied, handing him one of the wide brushes.

"The house is white."

"Very good, Judd. And the grass is green and the sky is blue."

"Surely you don't intend to paint the house blue." He looked at her in horror. "Farmhouses are white."

"Is that a state law, or only a rural ordinance?" Ginger asked, amused by his expression. She had tried to maintain distance from him since the night before, embarrassed at her display of emotion, the showing of her weakness. It had been very late when they had finally walked together to the house. They had gone directly to their own rooms, not speaking. And again this morning neither of them had acknowledged what had passed between them the night before.

But now, seeing his indignation at the idea of painting the house blue, she felt a small crack in her armor.

"I want it blue. Then I've been considering a sort of pale peach color for the barn." She kept her features carefully schooled.

"Pale peach…you want to paint the barn *peach?*" His dark eyebrows climbed so high, she feared they would fly right off the top of his head. "Barns are red. They are always red." He sighed in frustration. "Ginger, please…let's talk about this. I can live with a blue house if I have to, but don't make me live with a peach-colored barn."

Ginger seemed to contemplate his words, then nodded. "I think we can compromise. We'll paint the house blue and keep the barn its traditional red."

He grinned at her in obvious relief and dipped the tip of his paintbrush into the pale blue paint. He straightened up and eyed her suspiciously. "I think I've been had."

"What do you mean?" Ginger looked at him innocently.

"You never were thinking of painting the barn peach." It was a statement of fact.

She merely shrugged and smiled, then dipped her own brush into the can. "I'll start at the bottom and work up and you can start at the top and work down."

"Gee, thanks," he said dryly, looking up to the roof of the three-story farmhouse. "Here, hold this and I'll go get the extension ladder." He handed her his paintbrush, then took off in the direction of the barn.

She watched him go, her expression pensive. She had been so angry with him the night before, but this morning it was difficult for her to summon back that same emotion.

She couldn't forget the way he had held her. She'd felt as if she was falling into a dark pit, and he'd been the cushion to break her fall. He hadn't allowed their personal differences to interfere, he'd seen her need and he'd responded.

As he exited the barn, hefting the ladder over his shoulder, she whirled around and squatted down. She applied the brush to the base of the house, irritated by her mellow thoughts where Judd was concerned.

Nothing has changed between us, she thought, brushing on the paint with broad strokes. Just because he was kind to me last night doesn't mean we're suddenly going to become bosom buddies.

He'd stolen so much of her past, interfered in the relationship between her and her grandfather. A single night of him being kind to her couldn't erase years of unhappiness.

He set the ladder up near her, whistling softly beneath his breath. She handed him his paintbrush and watched as he grabbed a gallon of paint and ascended the ladder.

They worked silently for much of the morning. It was not an uneasy silence, nor was it a companionable one. It was merely the silence of two people working together but occupied with their own thoughts.

At noon Lisa brought out sandwiches and a pitcher of iced tea. "It's time for a break," she said, eyeing their progress so far. "It's looking good. I like the blue as a change from the white."

Ginger shot a triumphant look at Judd, then looked back at Lisa. "How are you feeling today?" Ginger asked. She took the lunch tray from Lisa and looked at her worriedly, noting that Lisa looked a little pale.

"Oh, I'm fine." Lisa waved her hands as if to dismiss Ginger's worries. "I think I ate too much the other night and paid with a day of indigestion."

"Anytime you don't feel well, don't come," Judd said as he climbed down the ladder. "Stay in bed and rest. Ginger and I can get along okay." Ginger nodded her agreement.

Lisa looked from Judd to Ginger, smiling in amusement. "Well, isn't this a red-letter day, the two of you agreeing with each other."

"On this particular topic, we do agree. Neither of us wants you trying to do too much," Ginger said, looking at Lisa fondly.

"Don't worry about me." She patted her big belly. "Junior and I are doing just fine. In fact, I'm going to go in now and put my feet up while you two eat lunch." With a parting smile, she turned and waddled back into the house.

"Why don't we eat over there in the shade?" Judd pointed to a large oak tree. Ginger nodded and followed him to the cool grass in the shade.

"Lisa's going to be a great mother," he said once they were settled, picking up one of the thick sandwiches and pouring them each a glass of the iced tea.

"Yes, she will." Ginger took the glass from him and sipped the cold tea. "There was a time when I went through a stage where I secretly pretended Lisa was my mother." Ginger smiled reflectively. "Of course, she didn't act like my mother so I had to concoct a fantasy to explain that. I worked it up in my head that Lisa had been in a terrible accident and had bumped her head and was suffering from amnesia. That's why she didn't act like my mom—she'd forgotten who she was." She colored slightly as she looked at Judd. "Pretty dumb, huh?"

"No, not dumb," he replied. He recognized it as the desire of a young girl to create a family to take the place of the one that had been taken away from her. "I did much the same thing, only in my case there was an older man I liked to pretend was my father."

"You didn't have a father when you were growing up?"

"When I was eight years old, my father decided he didn't like the responsibilities of wife and child. He left one day to get groceries, only he never came back." His voice grew harder and his eyes darkened. "It was a 'good riddance' situation. He wasn't exactly a *Father Knows Best* kind of dad.''

"What about your mom?" Ginger asked. She didn't want to stop the flow of conversation. Judd had never mentioned his family before, never discussed his past. He'd always acted as if his life had begun on the day he'd arrived at Serenity.

"Mom died when I was seventeen. She was an alcoholic." The words were uttered stiffly, devoid of emotion.

Ginger suddenly had a vision of his childhood, a bleak and unstable existence. No wonder he was reluctant to leave Serenity.

She shoved these thoughts aside. She wasn't responsible for his past, and she wouldn't become responsible for his future.

"Grandpa was really the only close family I had," she said, needing to remember the hurt she'd felt when Judd had come between her and her grandfather.

"Tom was the only close friend I had," he returned, his gaze not wavering from hers. His gray eyes were challenging, as if daring her to refute his words. She broke the gaze and turned her attention to her sandwich.

For a few minutes they ate in silence, the only sounds those of the farm life around them, the lowing of the cattle in the lower pasture, bird songs adding melody to the insects' resonant noise. Unlike the silence they had shared earlier, this one was charged with tension. The longer it lingered, the more oppressive it became.

Judd watched her with narrowed eyes as she ate. Why was it that every time Tom came up in conversation between them, Judd immediately felt her defenses rise, her hostility grow? How was it possible for the farm to prosper and grow if he and Ginger constantly fought? Tom would not have wanted it this way, nor did Judd. Somehow, someway, he and Ginger needed to establish some sort of truce.

"Ginger," he finally said, breaking the charged silence. "Can't you and I come to some sort of an understanding for the sake of Serenity? Must we always be at odds every time your grandfather's name comes up? Must he stand between us at every turn?"

"Not at all." She eyed him coolly. "Just keep in mind that he was your employer...he was my family." She stood up and brushed off the seat of her shorts. "It's time to get back to work."

Damn him, she thought as she worked her paintbrush back and forth, transforming white to pale, country blue. He was a crafty devil, lulling her into a false sense of camaraderie with his small insight into his past. All he wanted was to have his own way where the farm was concerned.

She watched him as he took their lunch tray back into the house, then returned to join her. They had come to a place where they were working at the same level, their shoulders almost, but not quite, touching. She felt irritation sweep over her as he paused a moment to pull off his T-shirt, then continued with his work. From the corner of her eye she could see his bronzed shoulder muscles flexing and rippling as he moved his paintbrush up and down.

She suddenly found herself remembering the kiss he'd given her on the day she had attempted to install the lock on her bedroom door. It had been a quicksilver kiss, barely long enough for the full effect to register on her. She now found herself wondering what it would be like to leisurely taste his lips, explore the contours of his smoothly muscled arms as they wrapped themselves around her.

Other memories from the past insinuated themselves in her brain. One night she had sneaked into his room, intent on pouring glue in his hair while he slept. She couldn't even remember how old she had been. But what she did remember was the moonlight streaming into his bedroom window…the warm glow of his naked, tanned skin…the matting of thick chest hair…

"Damn," she yelled in surprise as she felt a glob of paint splat on the top of her head.

"Sorry," Judd grunted from above her, watching as she stalked into the house. When she'd disappeared, he breathed a sigh of relief. He didn't like the way he was beginning to think about Ginger. He didn't like the way his thoughts kept lingering on the length of her tanned legs. He didn't like the way his mind was playing tricks on him, viewing and reviewing the scene of her in the bathtub, and each time he saw the scene, the bubbles in her bath had deteriorated a little bit more.

He had to find her a man. One thing Judd believed in was the sanctity of marriage, and he would never think of tilling another man's garden. If Ginger was married, then any temptation would be removed.

He was whistling tunelessly beneath his breath when she returned, her hair damp from her efforts to remove the paint he'd splattered.

"I think I'll work over here," she muttered, moving to the left of the ladder where she was out of his aim.

"I saw an old acquaintance of yours when I was in town the other day," Judd said.

She looked up at him with interest. "Oh, really? Who?"

"Roger Howell."

Ginger laughed, a spurt of spontaneous, melodious laughter that made Judd's heart perform a strange lurch in his chest.

"What's so funny?" he asked, surprised to realize it was the first time he'd heard her express joy since she'd been back on the farm.

"Oh, it's nothing." She laid down her paintbrush and leaned back on her haunches, amusement lifting the corners of her mouth and creating a bewitching twinkle in her eyes. "You know how sometimes people get frozen in your mind and no matter how they grow and change, no matter what they do with the rest

of their life, you have this single image of them that
supersedes any others?''

"I'm not sure I understand what you mean." Judd,
too, put down his paintbrush and leaned against the
ladder, enjoying the sunlight playing in the red curls
of her hair, the smile that made her achingly beautiful.

"Roger and I were in high school together," she
began, stifling another small burst of chuckles. "One
day a bunch of us were sitting at the lunch table and
somebody said something funny, and Roger laughed.
Unfortunately he had a mouthful of milk at the time."
She laughed again and shook her head. "Since then,
every time I think of him, I get this mental picture of
him with milk coming out of his nose."

Judd smiled thinly, mentally crossing the milk-
spurting Roger off his list. Still, despite his discour-
agement, he couldn't help but enjoy Ginger's laughter. "You should do that more often," he observed
softly.

"Do what?" She smiled up at him curiously.

"Laugh."

Like the last note of an echo, her smile faded. "I
haven't had too many reasons to laugh lately." She
picked up her paintbrush and redirected her attention
to her task.

For the rest of the afternoon they worked in silence, once again each withdrawing into the isolation
of private thoughts. Ginger tried to keep hers schooled
to neutral matters, refusing to consider how attrac-

tive Judd looked without his shirt. In fact, she tried to keep her gaze averted from him so as not to be distracted by the attractive width of his broad, tanned back. But no matter how hard she tried, her eyes kept returning to his physique, and the more she looked, the more irritated she became. Why did he have to work bare-chested? Granted it was warm, but the T-shirt he'd been wearing when the morning had begun wasn't exactly heavy material.

"Aren't you afraid of getting a sunburn?" she finally asked crossly.

"What?" he grunted, his humor obviously as ill as her own.

"Must you work without your shirt? It's so...coarse." She wrinkled her nose to display her distaste.

Judd stared at her blankly, as if not sure he'd understood what she'd said. He descended the ladder with slow, methodical movements, setting his paintbrush on one of the ladder rungs. He placed his hands on his hips and stared at her incredulously. "Does my bare chest bother you?"

"As a matter of fact, it does." She stood up and faced him, her eyes holding the familiar light of defiance.

His eyes were silver as he regarded her. "Just what is it about my bare chest that you object to?" His hand reached up and touched a tuft of the dark hair in the center of his chest.

"It's just too...too...bare." Ginger flushed hotly, sorry she'd even brought up the subject.

"While we're on the subject of bare, let's talk about those shorts of yours. Don't you think they're a little risqué?"

Ginger gasped at his effrontery. "There is nothing wrong with those shorts." She ran her hands down the sides of the cutoff denim shorts.

"Either those shorts are too short, or your legs are too long." His gaze now held open hostility, but beneath that emotion, Ginger sensed another. The nightgown in the bathroom, the perfume spritzed everywhere in the house, those things seemed to have little effect on him. But her shorts...oh, she saw the effect they were having on him. There was a sudden tension radiating from him, and his lips were set in a tight, grim line. His eyes were no longer a pale silver, but rather the color of hot, melted metal, and she felt a fire begin to burn deep within her.

Her mind whispered that she was treading into dangerous, uncharted territory, but she saw his weakness and wanted to exploit it. How long could a man be teased and frustrated? How long before he would finally pack his bags and leave?

She moved closer to him, wanting the danger, feeling her adrenaline pumping as she saw his eyes flicker with warning. She licked her lips, tasting the sweet flavor of success as she saw his eyes narrow and his body tense as if preparing for her assault. "So, which is it, Judd? Are my shorts too short or my legs too long?" She reached up to touch his chest, wanting to dance her fingers through his hair, test the strength of her power over him. Before her hand could touch him, he grabbed her wrist and pulled her up hard against the length of his body.

"What's your game, Paprika?" His voice was a tightly controlled growl. "Do you want to see how far you can push me? Do you want to know if I find you desirable?" His hands grabbed her hipbones and pressed her pelvis to his, making her aware of his arousal.

She gasped in shock, the depth of her own response stunning her. She wanted him. Oh, God, she wanted him. It wasn't supposed to be like this. And yet, she didn't want to fight the feelings that were overwhelming her. She closed her eyes, losing herself in a sensation of desire she had never known before.

She was vaguely aware of his muttered curse, then his lips were on hers, bruising hers as he pressed deeply, his tongue thrusting boldly.

Her tongue met his, touch for touch, thrust for thrust. She was out of control, not responsible for her hands, which moved convulsively across his naked chest, rubbing muscles, tangling in the hair, lingering over his nipples which hardened in response to her touch.

He gasped against her mouth, his breath hot and shuddering. His hands reached up and tangled in her hair, tugging her away from him.

She opened her eyes, dazed, squinting against the sunlight that pulled her out of the darkness of desire and back into the world of sanity. She saw his face above hers drawn with anger, hard with strain.

"Don't play the tease with me, Paprika," he said between clenched teeth. "You're out of your league." He released her completely, giving her a small push away from him.

As total sanity reclaimed her, Ginger took another step away from him, still stunned by her response to him. She stared at him in horror, realizing the weapon she had hoped to use on him had backfired. She'd hoped to use his desire for her against him, to drive him away. Now she was faced with an even bigger problem...what to do with the desire she felt for him.

"Judd, honey, isn't the pie any good?"

Judd looked up into Amanda's blue eyes, flushing as he realized his thoughts had been far away from her and her culinary delights.

"It's fine," he assured her, taking a big bite of the banana cream pie she'd baked just for him.

Amanda joined him on the flowered chintz sofa, her perfume a cloying cloud that preceded her. "Are you sure everything is all right? You seem so preoccupied." She trilled her musical laughter. "Silly me, you must be totally exhausted after painting all day long." She reached her hands up and moved them across Judd's taut neck muscles. "Poor dear. You're just a bundle of tightness. Why can't Ginger hire some professional to come paint the house?"

"Because painting and maintaining is my job. Besides, I'm fine," Judd said, moving out of her reach with a small smile. "You're right, I'm just tired." Actually he was not fine. He was confused as hell, and beginning to feel a little desperate. He felt like there was a storm brewing, a storm to end all others, a cataclysmic eruption of emotions that would leave both him and Ginger scarred and bleeding.

"I think I'll just head on back to the farm." He smiled apologetically at Amanda, who looked disappointed. "I'm really not fit company for anyone tonight." He stood up and headed toward the front door.

"We're still on for the dance this Friday night, aren't we?" she asked as they paused at her door.

"The dance?"

"At the Elk's Club."

"Oh sure," he said without enthusiasm, remembering he'd promised to take her. "I'll call you later in the week with the arrangements." He pecked the cheek she offered him, then escaped into the coolness of the night air.

Escape... funny, he'd never thought about needing to escape from Amanda before. But tonight, he'd felt claustrophobic in her small apartment with all her dainty lace doilies and delicate knickknacks. He'd felt smothered by her agreeable nature, her complacency, overwhelmed by her flagrant femininity.

He got into his pickup, frowning as he thought of the dance the next weekend. He was sorry now he'd invited Amanda. In fact, he was now beginning to remember why he had stopped seeing Amanda before. Boredom... pure and simple. Amanda was the most passive, helpless, boring female he'd ever known. She didn't stimulate him, didn't challenge him. She didn't invigorate him like...he stopped the thought before it could completely formulate.

He pressed on the gas pedal, his tumultuous thoughts racing ahead.

Judd had to find a man for Ginger. A man who could take her off his hands. Where in the hell was he going to find such a guy? Single men didn't exactly flock around the farm....

The dance! Of course, why didn't he think of it before? Everyone in town who was single always attended the shindigs at the Elk's Club. He'd take Ginger to the dance with Amanda. It would be a perfect opportunity for him to see Ginger interacting with some of the available men in town. Yes, it was a great idea.

He stifled a moan as he saw the flashing light of a patrol car behind him. He looked down at his speedometer and groaned even louder. Terrific, he was hitting seventy in a fifty-five zone. Damn, just what he needed, a speeding ticket. He pulled over to the side of the road, stepping out of the truck as a young, cleancut patrolman approached him.

If fate was kind, the police officer would be single and looking to marry a redheaded hellcat with cinnamon-colored eyes.

Chapter Six

Ginger paced the living room restlessly, trying to focus her attention on her sane thoughts rather than the insane. And there were plenty of crazy ones rattling around in her head. They'd been there ever since Judd had kissed her, forcing her to acknowledge her desire for him.

She'd turned and walked away that afternoon, escaping his heated gaze and her own inner turmoil. But now, alone with only the sounds of night outside the window, there was no place for her to run to get away from her reflections.

She wanted him. She couldn't deny it. She also realized that she could play no more games, take no more chances. She wasn't sure she could trust him, but she now knew she couldn't trust herself. If she fanned

the sparks that hid just beneath the surface between
herself and Judd, she couldn't trust herself to have the
willpower to douse the flame that might result. Any
physical relationship that might take place could never
be anything other than just that. There was too much
emotional baggage between them, too much distrust,
too many wounds.

Besides, Judd had made it abundantly clear that she
wasn't his type. He'd made it plain that he liked his
women soft and cuddly, complacent and even tem-
pered. Like Amanda Withers.

Ginger moved over to the window and stared out
into the darkness. Even as kids, Amanda and Ginger
had been total opposites. Amanda had been the kind
of girl who was always teacher's pet, dressed in ruffles and bows and with perfect blond curls. Amanda
was a follower, a people pleaser. Ginger, on the other
hand, was usually ordered to the corner of the
schoolroom for throwing spit balls or fighting. Any
ruffle was ripped, all bows lost. Ginger had little patience with silly rules and restrictions. The teachers
used to laugh that Ginger not only marched to a different drummer, she had her own band.

But Judd was spending most of his evenings with
Amanda. Apparently the colorless blonde had won his
heart. For some reason this thought depressed Ginger
enormously.

She turned away from the window and flopped
down on the sofa. The silence of the house pressed in
on her, making her aware of not only how alone she

was in the house, but in her life. She'd made no real friends when in New York, nor had she left any friends behind, here in Gentry. Her grandfather had always been enough. He'd always seemed so strong, so invincible. She'd never considered how lonely she'd be when he was gone.

It didn't seem fair that Judd wasn't as lonely as she. He professed to love her grandfather as much as she, but he was easing his loneliness in Amanda's arms.

It irritated Ginger that Judd could kiss her, talk about desiring her, then run to Amanda's place and expend that desire with Amanda. Ginger stoked the fire and Amanda got the heat . . . it infuriated Ginger.

She started as she heard a truck door slam, signaling that Judd was home. She looked down at her wristwatch. He was back earlier than usual. Perhaps there had been trouble in paradise. She didn't understand why this thought perversely pleased her.

The front door slammed and he appeared, looking like a thundercloud about to spew violence.

"What are you doing still up?" he growled, stalking across the room to the portable bar.

"I didn't realize I had a particular bedtime," she returned, watching while he fixed himself a scotch on the rocks. "While you're pouring, I'll take one . . . neat," she added, thinking a belt of scotch would relax her body, maybe numb her brain enough so she could sleep.

He poured a jigger of the burnished liquid into a small glass and carried it over to where she sat. He eased down next to her, his thigh brushing against hers as he settled into the overstuffed sofa. Ginger immediately felt an explosion of heat deep in her stomach. She moved her leg away, irritated that there seemed to be so much raw energy pulsating in the air. Before she hadn't recognized what was causing the tension, but now she knew exactly what it was. Sexual tension. The problem was that although she could now identify it, she didn't know what to do about it. She decided the best thing to do was try to ignore it.

"Tired?" she asked, seeing the lines of his face, lines that looked more deeply etched than they had earlier in the day. His strong lower jawline was darkened with a stubble of whisker growth, and she fought the impulse to reach out and run her hand down the roughness, feel it against her cheek.

"A little," he admitted, pausing to sip his scotch. "I got a speeding ticket on the way home."

"Gee, I'm so sorry."

He looked at her with a touch of amusement. "You don't sound sorry. In fact, you sound almost pleased."

She laughed, unable to deny it. "You always did have a lead foot."

"How would you know how fast I drive? It's been years since you've been in a vehicle with me."

They smiled at each other and Ginger knew he was remembering the last time they'd ridden together. She had been fifteen years old and her grandfather had insisted it would be good for her to attend a school dance. It had been one of the few times Tom had been adamant about making her do something she didn't want to do. Judd had been assigned the task of driving her into town.

"I may have been heavy on the gas pedal, but you were definitely fleet of foot."

She grinned. "I warned you that the first time you stopped the car I was going to jump out and run back to the farm."

"And I warned you that if you did, I'd catch you and whip the tar out of you."

Ginger giggled. "It's a good thing you didn't catch me."

They smiled again. This time their smiles held nothing more than the warmth of shared memories, the nostalgia of crazy days of youth now passed and never to be revisited.

"I suppose there were times when I was a bit of a handful," she conceded grudgingly.

"I can't remember any time that you weren't a handful." Judd chuckled, a sound as pleasant as deep-toned wind chimes floating on a breeze. "I will say this, you kept life interesting for me. I got up each morning wondering what sort of mischief you'd planned that day for me. You never disappointed me."

Ginger smiled and tucked her feet up beneath her. "Grandpa would have skinned me alive if he'd known about the molasses in your dresser drawers." She looked at Judd, curious as a sudden thought struck. "Why didn't you tell on me? There were lots of times

I did some terrible things to you, but you never breathed a word to Grandpa. Why?"

He shrugged and paused a moment to sip his drink. "I don't know, maybe there was a part of me that admired your spunk. Maybe I commended your deviousness—and you *were* devious." He paused, then added, "Or maybe I'm just a masochist at heart."

"I doubt that," she laughed, then sobered slightly. "Still, I suppose I should apologize for some of the things I did." She grinned at him impishly. "But I won't, because at the time I thought you deserved everything I did to you."

"I'm glad you're not apologizing to me. You wouldn't want to ruin your image as a hell-raiser."

"On that note, I think I'll go on up to bed. You want this?" She held out her drink, which she hadn't touched. She didn't need it anymore. She felt relaxed by their easy conversation, mellowed by the memories.

"No thanks. I think I'll hit the hay, too." He stood up with her and drained his glass, then carried his and Ginger's to the bar.

"Don't forget the chicks are being delivered early tomorrow morning," he reminded her.

"How can I forget. I hate chickens." She made a face to express her sentiments.

He chuckled. "You'll get used to them."

"I suppose that's true. I hate you and I'm starting to get used to you," she said with a giggle. He laughed, too, letting her know he wasn't angry at her words.

Judd shut off the light in the living room and together they climbed the stairs.

"Goodnight, Judd," she said as they came to her bedroom door.

"Goodnight, Paprika. Pleasant dreams." As he continued on to his own room, Ginger entered hers and closed the door behind her. She wasn't sure exactly what had just happened between them. But somehow they had managed to put their animosity, their intense awareness of each other aside and simply enjoy each other's company. She didn't know exactly what had caused the change between them, but she hoped it continued.

"Oh, they're so cute," Ginger exclaimed, laughing at the little chicks that filled the floor of the brooder house.

Judd smiled at her, watching as she bent down and picked up one of the little birds. "Don't get too attached to him, someday he might be somebody's Sunday dinner main course."

She nodded, putting the chick back down. She'd long ago learned the realities of farm life. Her grandfather had warned her about the heartache of becoming fond of a particular animal.

She looked over to where Judd was checking the brooder warming lights. Speaking of becoming fond of a particular animal... She smiled wryly.

The easy camaraderie that had sprung up between them the night before had continued into the morning, bringing with it a relieving of the tenseness, an easing of taut nerves. It was strange and somehow pleasant, this new, tentative truce between them.

"So, what happens now?" she asked when he was finished checking the lights and they left the brooder house.

"The chicks stay there for about the next month. Once they're fully feathered, we put them out in the pen," he explained.

"You mean when they get big and ugly, they go out into the pen." She smiled and continued. "I thought most poultry farms kept their chickens in little cages."

"Ah, but that's where Serenity chickens will be different. We're going to raise ours the old-fashioned way. Your grandpa wanted them raised the way God intended, pecking and scratching on the ground. No cages, no chemicals, only fresh air, sunshine and all natural grains." Judd's face took on a youthful animation. "I've already set everything up with a packager and a distributor." In his enthusiasm, he grabbed both her hands in his. "It's a bit of a gamble, Ginger, but I think this venture will make Serenity successful beyond our wildest expectations."

"From the portfolio Mr. Roberts showed me, I thought Serenity was already pretty successful."

He released her hands as they resumed walking toward the house. "Yes, Serenity looks pretty successful on paper, but most of the wealth is tied up in farm machinery and the land. If you were to liquidate your assets, you'd be fairly comfortable, but to continue Serenity as a working farm, you're just keeping your head above water.'' As they reached the barn, he sat down on the top railing of the fence that surrounded the red building. Ginger leaned against the fence next to him. ''I want Serenity successful enough, wealthy enough so that we never have to worry about it being taken away from us.''

His voice was so filled with emotion that Ginger knew he wasn't conscious of his use of the plural 'us.' ''It's so important to you, this farm?''

He didn't answer for a long moment. He stared off into the distance, and when he did finally speak, Ginger knew he was far away in his distant past. ''I was born on a farm,'' he began, his voice holding the quality of somebody remembering painful times. ''It was a small farm just outside Kansas City. My dad wasn't a good farmer, but he was a lucky man. When he left, there was enough money in the bank to keep the place going for a couple of years. Unfortunately my mom wasn't emotionally stable enough to manage the place. She suffered bouts of deep depression.'' He broke off, his voice full, as if the memories were too painful to speak aloud. When he did finally talk again, he sounded stiff and unnatural, as if he was reading from a bad script. ''When I was twelve, we lost the farm. I didn't realize how much of my soul I'd put into that place. After Dad left, Mom seemed like such a stranger. The only thing familiar and sane was the land. I knew it would never leave me, it would never betray me. Then even it was gone. We moved into a dumpy little apartment near the stockyards. After that, Mom didn't even pretend to fight her depression. She jumped into a bottle of booze and never climbed out.''

Ginger laid her hand on his arm, seeing the pain he'd always guarded so closely, her heart crying for the little boy he had once been. ''So young to be coping with so much,'' she murmured.

He smiled jauntily, his face wearing the mask of a man who didn't want to expose his pain, reveal his weaknesses. ''It wasn't so bad. At least I had Tom.''

''My grandpa?'' she asked, looking at him in astonishment. ''But I thought you met him the day you arrived here and Grandpa hired you.''

Judd shook his head. ''I met Tom when I was thirteen. I spent most of my time hanging out at the stockyards, listening to the farmers talk and exchange ideas. I met your grandpa there.''

''He was the man you mentioned yesterday... the one you used to pretend was your father?'' Ginger's world tilted just a little bit as he nodded affirmatively. It seemed strange to her to realize that her grandfather had not only fulfilled an important role in her life, but in Judd's life, as well. And she hadn't even been aware of it.

''Your grandpa used to come to town one weekend a month. God,'' he breathed, smiling boyishly. ''I lived for those weekends. Tom would take me out for a big steak dinner and he'd talk to me like I was his equal . . . like I was important. He told me all about Serenity, and I dreamed about one day coming here, sharing it all with Tom." He flushed, as if embarrassed by his openness.

Ginger was silent, fighting a myriad of emotions. She now understood more clearly his commitment to Serenity. And she could no longer doubt the fact that Judd had cared for her grandfather. But there was a small part of her, a parentless little girl, who wondered if she hadn't been cheated. Had Judd's intrusion into their lives caused her grandfather to give him some of the love, some of the affection that might otherwise have been hers alone? And even with her new understanding of Judd, there was still an underlying anger that he hadn't tried hard enough to contact her when her grandfather had died. It had taken him three days to reach her, then it had been too late for her to make the arrangements to get back in time for the funeral.

Still, it was too nice a day to summon the anger to confront him with this. She was enjoying too much the tenuous truce they were experiencing.

"Come on, Lisa should have lunch ready about now."

He nodded and jumped off the fence and together they walked toward the house. "There's a dance this Friday night at the Elk's Club," he said. "I'm going and I was wondering if you'd like to go, too."

The invitation came as a total surprise, attesting to the newfound relationship being formed between them.

"Okay," she agreed, surprised by the pleasure that swept through her at the thought of attending the dance with him.

"There's only one thing you have to promise me." He grinned at her.

"What's that?"

"That you won't jump out of the truck and run back here."

Ginger laughed. "I promise," she readily agreed, wondering why she suddenly felt so happy.

"Come on, Ginger. The dance will be half over before we even get there," Judd yelled up the stairs.

"Just a minute, I'll be right down," she answered.

Judd looked at his wristwatch, then patted his shirt breast pocket, checking to make sure he had the small notebook that contained his list of prospective husbands for Ginger. He was feeling confident, sure of the master plan he'd devised. Any man who expressed an interest in Ginger at the dance, any man she showed an interest in, was going on his list. Surely there would be some male at the dance who could put up with her streak of stubbornness and redheaded temper. Surely there was a man in the town of Gentry who could love her despite her faults.

"Hey, Ginger," he called up the stairs again, impatient to leave. As it was, he was already ten minutes late to pick up Amanda. And he had a feeling Amanda was not going to be thrilled when she saw Ginger in the truck. He'd told neither woman that the other was going. In Amanda's case, he hadn't wanted to hear her whine or pout, and in Ginger's case he didn't figure it mattered.

He looked again at his watch and sighed impatiently. The sigh caught in his throat as she appeared at the top of the staircase. She was a kaleidoscope of colors, a vibrant rainbow in motion as she skipped down the steps.

The spaghetti-strapped bodice was lemon yellow, contrasting pleasingly with the tan she'd picked up over the past couple of days. From the cinched waist, the dress exploded into ruffles of brilliant colors—orange, red, purple—ending in a skimpy length well above her knees. Her feet were adorned with bright yellow high heels that emphasized the long shapeliness of her legs. She looked so alive, so vibrant, so desirable...Judd felt an ache in his groin, a need long denied attempting to be acknowledged.

"It's about time," he snapped, anger his defense against unwanted emotions. Without waiting for her, he grabbed his keys off the end table and headed for the front door.

Ginger followed him hesitantly, sorry that their night was beginning on a sour note. Maybe it's the dress that set him off, she thought. It was a bit bold, extremely festive. But she'd been in a festive mood all day, like a small child anticipating a birthday party, and she'd wanted her clothes to reflect her mood.

"I should have worn a shroud," she muttered as she hurried to catch up with him.

Judd had expected her to snap back at him. He was surprised when instead she slid into the truck, her eyes holding the dimmed light of the wounded.

He'd only driven a little ways when he could stand it no longer. Her silence played on his nerves, stimulated his guilt. "I'm sorry I snapped at you," he finally said.

"I'm sorry I made you wait for me," she replied.

He smiled. "It was worth the wait. You always did clean up real nice."

"You don't look half bad yourself," she returned lightly. Actually, he looked great. He wore a pair of black dress slacks and a pale gray shirt that exactly matched his eyes. He looked sophisticated and confident, able to hold his own in any crowd. It was only when you looked deep in his eyes that you sensed the whisper of danger, the depth of emotion he kept well guarded. They were the eyes of a man who knew what he wanted and would go after it with energy and passion.

Ginger had a feeling that she and Judd were kindred spirits. Had they not been cast in adversarial positions so long ago, they might have been friends. She had a feeling that he was one of the few people who could meet her, will for will—match her, temper for temper.

"Why haven't you married?" The question popped out of her mouth before she realized she was going to ask it.

He looked at her in surprise. As he mulled the question over in his mind, he realized he had no real answer for her other than the obvious. "I suppose because I've never found a woman I can't live without." He wouldn't, couldn't tell her that he'd always been just a little bit afraid to trust in the emotion of love. He'd lost at it so many times before.

"You haven't ever been in love?"

Judd grinned humorlessly. "It's been my experience that there's not much longevity in love. People walk out, they give up, they die. People don't last. But the land, it lasts forever."

Ginger found his words sad testimony to his difficult youth. She, too, had little longevity when it came to relationships. Her grandfather had been the only constant in her life, and now he was gone. But where Judd had apparently decided not to trust his heart to love, Ginger longed for love. She wanted someone to share her life with, someone to laugh with on sunny days, somebody who would hold her close on stormy nights.

Still, despite their differences, each time she was with Judd she learned a little bit more about him. Each time, he exposed a touch more of the inner man, and it was a far cry from the cold, mocking, opportunity-seeking man she'd once imagined him to be.

"The land makes a pretty cold bedfellow," she finally said softly.

He grinned at her, his eyes a pale silver in the light from the dashboard. "I've never had any problems finding warm bedmates."

"I'm sure you haven't," she returned coolly, irritated to feel a small stab of jealousy at the thought of him in some woman's bed. "But then there are some women who like sleeping with snakes."

He chuckled. "Now there's the Paprika I know and love."

Her anger waned just as quickly as it had appeared, and she returned his grin. She didn't want to fight with him, not tonight. She wanted...strange, she wasn't sure what she wanted where he was concerned anymore.

She now looked over to him, studying his profile in the dim car lighting. There was no denying she found him physically attractive. With his thick dark hair and bold features he was an exceedingly handsome man. Yes, she'd accepted the fact that she was physically drawn to him. What bothered her was that there seemed to be something more drawing her to him, something deeper, more profound than mere physical attraction.

On impulse she reached over and laid her hand on his arm. "Thanks for asking me to come with you tonight. It will be good to see some of my old friends." She smiled at him. "Are you a good dancer?"

"I do everything well."

Ginger laughed. "You're especially good at humility."

"I learned it from a little girl I once knew." He looked at her, his gaze as warm as a summer breeze on naked flesh.

Ginger returned his gaze, trying to imagine what it would feel like to dance with him, to feel his strong arms enfold her, feel his heartbeat against her own. She didn't want him to think of the little girl she had once been. She wet her lips with the tip of her tongue, her mouth suddenly dry as a strange tension filled the truck. "In case you haven't noticed, the little girl is all grown up," she replied.

"I've noticed." His arm tensed beneath her hand.

The moment was broken as he made a right turn. "Where are you going? I thought the Elk's Club was to the left," Ginger said curiously.

"It is, but I've got to pick up Amanda."

"Amanda?" Shock reverberated inside her as she digested his words. Along with the shock came a surging of anger. How dare he? How dare he not tell her right up front that his date for the evening was Amanda, and she was merely a third wheel.

As Judd pulled up in front of Amanda's house, Ginger fought her impulse to jump out of the truck and run back to the farm. Her eyes narrowed as she watched Judd walk up the sidewalk to the front door. Amanda greeted him at the door, wearing a frothy, pink concoction that looked as if it would melt in the heat. No, Ginger thought watching the two of them approach the truck. She wasn't going to run back to the farm. There was no way she was going to allow Mr. Macho and the pink cream puff to ruin her fun tonight.

Chapter Seven

"Judd honey, don't you want to dance?" Amanda purred, leaning across the table and running her pointy, pink index fingernail up his forearm.

"I don't feel like dancing," Judd replied, moving his arm out of Amanda's reach.

Her lower lip protruded into a pout. "I thought we came here to have a good time. I didn't know you were going to sit and glower all night."

"I'm not glowering," he protested. "I just don't feel like dancing."

"But everyone is dancing," Amanda exclaimed, her voice like the whine of a small-engined motorcycle. "Everyone is having a good time except us. Look at Ginger, she's danced almost every dance."

Every dance except one, Judd thought sourly, his gaze focused on the red-haired belle of the ball. From the moment they had walked in the door of the Elk's Club, the single men had flocked around Ginger like cattle to a salt lick. It was disgusting, grown men acting so silly over a red-haired hellion who just happened to have the sexiest legs, the shapeliest figure and most flirtatious smile in the whole room. And why did she have to dance that way, hips shaking, body swaying, head thrown back to expose the graceful curve of her neck?

As the song on the jukebox came to an end, Judd watched as one man found Ginger a chair and three others rushed to the bar apparently to get her a drink. It was like a scene from *Gone With the Wind*, Ginger in the role of Scarlett O'Hara, holding court with her admirers.

Judd had begun the evening concentrating on who seemed to be attracted to Ginger, mentally adding their names to the list in his notebook. But as the evening progressed, he found himself discounting each and every single man in the room. They were all like mindless sheep, hypnotized by her enchanting smile, enthralled by her vivid coloring and liveliness. These men would not be good as husband material, not for a woman like Ginger. She needed somebody who could meet her, strength for strength, wit to wit.

Ginger needed a man strong enough to deal with her weaknesses, and weak enough to love her strengths.

Judd had to face the fact—Tom had given him an impossible assignment.

"I just don't understand you, Judd. Why did you come tonight if you didn't intend to have a good time?" The engine whine in Amanda's voice intensified.

"I'm having a good time." Judd looked at the woman next to him, then back at Ginger, who was once again out on the dance floor. It was like looking at a common moth, then being captivated by the vibrancy of an exotic butterfly.

"Well, if you aren't going to dance with me, maybe I should just go find somebody who will," Amanda said, the whine gone, replaced by childish petulance.

"Maybe that's a good idea," Judd replied, not wanting to be unkind, but realizing this would be his last date with her. He didn't want a woman like Amanda. He wanted . . . he clenched his jaw tightly, refusing to complete the thought. His gaze once again went to the redhead out on the dance floor.

"Come on, Ginger. Why won't you agree to go out with me next weekend?"

Ginger looked up at the attractive man she was dancing with, giving him the benefit of her wide smile. "Why Billy Wayne Green, I'm surprised that you'd even want me to. It seems to me that I remember before I left for New York, you liked to refer to me as a chili pepper—hot-tempered and skinny."

"Ah, Ginger, we were just kids then. Surely you aren't going to hold that against me," Billy Wayne protested, his handsome face creased with a frown.

"No, but I'm not going to hold anything else against you, either," Ginger muttered beneath her breath.

"What did you say?" Billy Wayne looked at her quizzically.

"Nothing." Ginger shook her head and indicated that the music was too loud for further conversation. As she danced, she studied the attractive, blond-haired man who was her partner. While growing up, she'd always had a bit of a crush on Billy Wayne Green. With his clean-cut features and golden hair, everyone had a little crush on him, including Billy Wayne himself. She should feel a bit of excitement that her childhood heartthrob was practically begging her to go out with him, but she felt nothing. There was only one man in the entire room who made a throb of excitement drum in her stomach.

She shot a glance at Judd, noting that he now sat at the table alone and the pink fluff was dancing with Harvey Lee, Gentry's senior banker. Ginger wondered if that was what was making Judd glower as if he'd just discovered a fox in his precious chicken coop. Then, deciding she didn't care what caused his deep frown, she grinned up at Billy Wayne until the music came to an end.

"Thanks for the dance," she said as they left the floor and headed for the bar.

"So, Ginger, you never answered me," Billy Wayne said as she grabbed a cold beer and drank deeply. "Are you going to go out with me or not?" He reached up and carefully patted his hair, as if wanting to make sure it still retained it's perfect plastic look. It did.

"Not," Ginger answered, but with a friendly smile. "But thanks, anyway." She looked at him firmly, letting him know her mind couldn't be changed.

Billy Wayne shrugged, then moved away, apparently in search of somebody who would more fully appreciate his charm.

Ginger pulled up a stool and sat down, enjoying the taste of her cold beer. Better slow down, girl, she told herself, feeling the noticeable glow the beer was producing. This was her third drink, and she knew better than anyone that she had absolutely no tolerance for beer. Still, the feeling was not unpleasant.

She looked over at Judd, her breath catching in her throat as their gazes locked across the crowded room. A moment might have passed, or an eternity might have slipped by as their eyes held, drawing them to each other although neither of them moved physically.

Desire . . . she saw it blazing in his smoldering eyes, making tendrils of heat unfurl in the pit of her stomach. She instantly remembered the way his lips had felt on hers, the feel of his naked chest beneath her fingertips. His eyes were telling her he remembered as well. The dark orbs radiated smoke and fire, causing goosebumps to dance on her spine and raise on her arms.

She snapped her head back around, breaking the gaze, realizing her hand was shaking as she brought the beer bottle back up to her lips. Damn him, he had no right to be flashing her his bedroom eyes. He should be flashing them at the woman he'd brought as his date.

"Ginger?"

She turned at the shy, hesitant voice and smiled at the thin, bespectacled man standing next to her.

"Why, Ronnie McKay. I didn't know you were still around. I figured you'd be on Wall Street setting the world of finance on its ears."

"Ah, not me," Ronnie blushed, reminding Ginger of the boy he had been. Serious minded, a genius at math, Ronnie had been something of a nerd, but he had always been kind to Ginger, a fact she hadn't forgotten.

"I was . . . uh . . . wondering if you'd like to dance," Ronnie stuttered as a slow song began to play on the jukebox.

"I'd love to." Ginger quickly downed the last of her beer. As she got down from the stool, she stumbled slightly, realizing that last beer had taken a direct route to her head.

She moved into Ronnie's arms, leaning against him a bit more than she normally would have as she struggled to get her equilibrium. As she and Ronnie began to move to the music, she noted that he was blushing again. Even the tips of his ears had turned to the color of overripe tomatoes. Poor Ronnie, it must be miserable to be so shy.

She squeaked in surprise as he suddenly pulled away from her and Ginger saw Judd standing next to them, his face the mask of an angry Aztec god. "I'm cutting in," Judd said, his voice a low, deep rumble.

Ronnie didn't try to object, he merely stepped aside and Judd took his place. Where Ronnie's arms around her had been hesitant and tentative, Judd's were firm and sure. He held her so close that a whisper couldn't make its way between them. His fingers splayed on her back, playing havoc with the surface temperature of her skin. Ginger's head was spinning, whether from the alcohol or from his nearness, she didn't know. She only knew she wanted the song to play forever, the dance to last an eternity. She wanted to remain in his arms until everyone else got tired and went home, leaving her and Judd alone together.

Judd was caught up in an emotional tailspin. She was warm against him, her scent surrounding him. He'd watched her in the arms of the other men until he could stand it no longer. His blood had pounded in his temples until he thought he'd go blind or insane. But now, holding her, the pounding had stopped, and instead the blood now surged powerfully through his veins, singing with the joy of holding her close.

"You were right earlier when you said you were a good dancer," she said, her voice a husky whisper in his ear.

"I told you I do everything well," he replied, loving the way the skin of her back felt beneath his hand.

"Shouldn't you be dancing with Amanda?" She cocked her head back and looked up at him. "Isn't it rude not to dance with your date for the evening?"

"I'm surprised you can dance at all. I know how exhausting it is to make a spectacle of yourself." His voice was harsher than he'd intended, the anger he'd always used as a defense there to serve him.

"A spectacle?" Ginger's eyes narrowed and the fires within began to flame a little brighter. "You might consider it a spectacle, I consider it fun."

"You find teasing fun?" His words caused her body to vibrate in his arms. "Poor innocent Ronnie was about to burst from your teasing ways."

"I wasn't teasing anyone," she returned succinctly.

"What do you call it? Flipping your skirt up, showing off your sexy legs." Again the anger was in his voice.

"You really think so?" She looked up at him once again, her fingers finding the hair that lay at the nape of his neck.

"Damn right, it's nothing but teasing."

She smiled at him. "I mean, do you really think my legs are sexy?" She twirled the thick hair on his neck, surprised to find it rich and silky to her touch.

"Don't try to change the subject," he retorted. "And stop doing that to my hair." His jaw muscles worked overtime, knotting and reknotting, and once again she noticed the stubby growth of whiskers that darkened his chin. "I think it's time we call it a night."

"You mean go home?" She stopped moving and looked at him in surprise. "But it's not that late."

"You're half-tipsy, and it's time to leave."

"If you want to leave, then go ahead and go. I can find a ride home." Ginger stared at him defiantly. "I'm sure Billy Wayne would be happy to give me a lift back to the farm."

"You came with me, and you're leaving with me." As the song came to an end, Judd fastened his hand on her arm in a tight grip and began to lead her to the door.

"What about Amanda?" Ginger asked containing her anger, saving it up until they got home. Then she was going to explode at his high-handed treatment.

"Harvey is taking Amanda home," he said, not releasing her arm until they were outside and standing next to the truck.

So that's why he's angry, Ginger thought, sliding into the front seat. But that gave him no right to drag her out and demand she leave. She glared at him as he got behind the wheel and started the engine.

The ride home was accomplished in silence. The closer they got to the farm, the angrier Ginger became. Who did he think he was, to call her a tease and act like a caveman? What right did he have to tell her what to do?

She held tightly to her anger, as always finding it more comfortable than the other emotions racing through her. It wasn't until they entered the house that Ginger let her rage loose. She turned around and faced Judd, her eyes blazing with the heat of a furnace fully stoked, making Judd's adrenaline and a sense of anticipation shudder through him.

"What gives you the right to give me orders and drag me out of the dance?"

"Somebody has to watch over you…you've got no sense," Judd returned, the blood once again pounding at his temples. "Your grandfather would have horsewhipped you if he'd watched you tonight, leading all those men on a merry chase."

"I was just having a good time," Ginger protested. "Would you prefer I simper around and play coy?" She moved across the room, executing a perfect imitation of Amanda's mincing walk. She stopped when she was directly before him. She batted her long lashes and reached up to touch the shirt button in the middle of his chest. "Judd, honey, can I bake you a pie? Darn your socks?"

"Knock it off, Ginger," Judd warned softly.

The warning went unheeded. She moved her hands up around his neck, feeling the taut muscles of his shoulders. "Oh Judd, sugar, you're all tense and knotted. Let me massage your muscles, let me give you a back rub. You know my only desire is to please you, accommodate your needs." She batted her eyelashes again in a perfect parody of Amanda.

Despite his anger, Judd chuckled. "You really are a little witch."

Ginger twisted away from him, feeling a strange sort of frustration seething inside. "So, I'm a teasing, tipsy witch. You'd better watch out, Judd, your compliments are liable to go right to my head." She walked over to the bar and poured herself a short scotch.

"You really think you should add that on top of those beers?" He watched her, captivated by the way the light in the room seemed to be skipping through her flame-colored hair, illuminating each strand into shining copper. His eyes narrowed as she glared at him defiantly, then tipped the glass up and swallowed the scotch in one shot.

"You are the most perverse woman I've ever known. You'd cut off your own nose if you thought it would spite my face." Judd felt his ire rising once again, like a tide washing over him, carrying his good sense out to sea. "You'll probably never find a man who'll put up with you. You're too damned contrary."

"Well, excuse me, Mister Perfect." Ginger slammed her glass down on the top of the bar. "It wasn't my date who went home with somebody else."

In three long strides Judd was before her, his eyes answering the blaze in hers. "You little fool, do you really think I give a damn who took Amanda home?" As Judd lowered his head and claimed Ginger's lips, he realized that what he thought had been rage was nothing of the kind. Desire, that's what he'd been feeling, frustrated desire that masqueraded as rage. But as he tasted her lips, savoring the sweetness with the provocative tang of warm scotch, the mask of anger fell away, leaving the blatant desire that burned through him.

With a low, guttural moan, he wrapped his arms around her, pulling her to him, chest to breast, hip to hip. The kiss was deep, hungry, attesting to the emotional status they'd both been in before the kiss had begun.

Judd knew someplace deep inside that he'd lost his mind. But if this was what it felt like to be insane, then he'd be happy to stay crazy for the remainder of his life.

His hands moved up to tangle in her hair, loving the feel of its short length caressing his hands. Molten silk, he thought, smelling the fresh scent of the red-gold strands.

He left her hair, his fingers traveling slowly down her back, then cupping her buttocks, pulling her closer... closer...

Ginger was lost. She had been from the moment his lips had claimed hers. The entire evening, the flirting, the dancing, the anger, all had merely been a prelude to this moment of being in Judd's arms.

His body heat surrounded her, invaded her, making her want more. The stubby whiskers were slightly rough against her skin, but it was a teasing, pleasing sensation. Her fingers worked to unbutton his shirt, wanting to feel the heat of his flesh against her. When she finished, she pulled at the shirt impatiently, struggling to ease it off his broad shoulders. As the shirt fell to the floor, she ran her palms across his tanned expanse of chest, loving the feel of sinewy muscle beneath the heat of his skin.

There had been a time when she had been a teenager and the sight of his bare chest had evoked alien emotions in her, feelings that had been frightening. But now she knew what those emotions were...a woman's desire for a man. She wanted him and she was beyond fear.

As his hands moved up her back, slowly...sensually, then upward to caress her breasts, she gasped with pleasure. Her lips parted and she tipped her head back to look at him, knowing her eyes were communicating her want, her need for him.

Judd looked into her eyes, seeing her acquiescence there. He knew then that he could take her, and God, how he wanted her. But as he stared into her eyes, a vision of Tom entered his mind. Tom had trusted him to look after Ginger, to take care of her. The promise Judd had made to the old man did not include making love to his granddaughter. Passion ebbed as guilt consumed. With a strength born of desperation, Judd pulled away and turned his back to her. "Go to bed, Ginger." His voice was low and dull.

"Judd?" Her hand was warm and inviting on his back, her uncertainty evident in her voice.

"Go to bed," he thundered.

For the first time in her life, Ginger did as she was told.

When she had left the room, leaving behind only a lingering trace of her evocative perfume, Judd expelled a ragged sigh.

Chapter Eight

Ginger had no idea why she obeyed him without an argument. Perhaps it was the utter starkness in his voice as he ordered her to her room. More likely it was because she herself had felt a sudden need to run...escape from him and all the things he made her feel.

However, she quickly discovered that her room hadn't been far enough for her to escape the myriad of emotions causing chaos in her head.

Her entire body felt like one huge nerve ending, raw and pulsating. She was like an electric guitar, all plugged in and tuned up, but with nobody to play the melody that ached deep within.

With numbed legs she moved across the bedroom, taking off her dress and changing into her nightclothes. She shut off her light and got into bed, hoping that by lying very still her head would stop spinning and she could make some sense out of things.

Desire, yes that was an emotion easily identified. Her swollen lips attested to it, the hunger deep in the pit of her stomach whispered it. But it was all mixed up with other, more subtle emotions.

Somewhere in the last week or two, Judd had crossed the line from adversary to friend. Granted, their friendship was a tenuous thing, forged by common interests and a growing sense of respect for each other.

She'd spent the evening surrounded by the most eligible bachelors the town of Gentry had to offer, and yet none of them had moved her at all. It had been the same way when she'd been living back in New York. Her aunt had played matchmaker, setting her up with dozens of young men, but none of them had done a thing for her.

The only man who had managed to deeply touch her was Judd. He was the only one who could evoke such a gamut of emotions—anger, grief, desire, laughter... She'd shared it all with him.

She rolled over on her back, watching the patterns the moonlight painted on the ceiling. She was confused, and with each moment that passed, her thinking grew fuzzier. She closed her eyes, thinking it would be best if she sorted everything out in the morning.

Ginger groaned before she even opened her eyes, knowing that the beer that had made her thinking so cloudy the night before had now created in her body a state of rebellion. She had a feeling that if she opened her eyes, she would be blinded by the headache that throbbed just behind her eyeballs.

That final scotch...the one she'd tossed back in direct defiance of Judd...that's the one that had done it. When would she learn that these childish actions hurt nobody but herself?

She winced as a soft knock sounded on her door. "Come in," she breathed, hoping it wasn't Judd. She wasn't ready to face him yet. She still needed to sort out her feelings where he was concerned. She cracked an eyelid and breathed a sigh of relief as Lisa walked in, carrying a steaming cup of coffee.

"Ah, you're a life saver," Ginger exclaimed, easing up to a sitting position and reaching up to grab her pounding head before it rolled off her shoulders.

"Judd said you might need a caffeine kick this morning." Lisa handed Ginger the coffee and held out two white tablets. "He also suggested you take two of these."

"What are they?" Ginger asked suspiciously.

"Extra-strength aspirin."

Ginger took them and swallowed them down with a gulp of the coffee, then leaned back against the wooden headboard and studied Lisa, who was rubbing the small of her back with one hand. "Are you feeling all right?"

Lisa nodded. "Just fine. But this little critter has been riding low the last couple of days, really dealing my back fits."

At the moment Ginger envied Lisa more than anyone she'd ever known. The woman glowed with her husband's love and with the new life that grew within her. "Lisa . . . how did you know that you were in love with Ray?"

She smiled and sat down on the edge of Ginger's bed. "When I first met Ray, I thought he was the most obnoxious man I'd ever seen. I couldn't see how anyone could live with him. Then, as I got to know him, I began to realize that I didn't want to live without him. That's love, Ginger, when you know you want to wake up every morning and see his face first, and you know he's the one you want to be with every night before you go to sleep."

Yes . . . Ginger had known for some time that she was in love with Judd, she just hadn't wanted to face it. She wondered if it had been there all along, even years ago when she'd thought she disliked him. Had that been what had chased her away? She had been too emotionally immature to deal with the feelings she had then, but now, she could no longer deny what was in her heart.

"You love Judd." It was not a question. Lisa smiled. "I've watched you with him, Ginger. I've seen you growing, flourishing with him."

"He makes me so angry," Ginger mused.

Lisa nodded. "Of course. Judd can make you angrier than anyone, and he can also hurt you more than anybody else. Your love gives him that power over you." Lisa reached out and put her arm around Ginger. "But the flip side of that is that he can give you the greatest happiness, make you feel better than anyone else in the world." Lisa hugged Ginger and gave a laugh of pure delight. "I love you and I love Judd more than anyone else I know. I'm so very happy that things are working out for the two of you."

"Whoa, slow down." Ginger pulled away from Lisa with a frown. "I know how I feel, but I don't have any idea how Judd feels about me."

Lisa smiled. "Then isn't it about time you found out?"

Judd walked through the gate of the small graveyard, noting how kind spring was, decorating the area with hundreds of wildflowers. Weeping willow trees lined one side of the wrought-iron fencing, their heads bent as if mourning the family members who rested here.

Even so, Judd had never found this cemetery a sad place. Rather he viewed it as a testimony to continuity.... Ginger's parents were here, along with her grandparents and their parents. Her heritage was in this land, and hopefully some day her great-grandchildren would come to this place to find peace and solace among the spirits of those who had lived before.

However, today Judd could find no peace. The events of the previous evening kept playing and replaying in his mind. It had been a sleepless night, one of guilt and self-recriminations.

He'd almost made an unthinkable mistake last night. He'd almost given in to his desire to make love to Ginger. It would have been unforgivable.

He'd promised Tom he'd find a good husband for Ginger, but Judd's own desire kept getting in the way. Seeing her last night, dancing in the arms of all those men, had made jealousy sweep over him. It had been a strange emotion, one he'd never experienced before.

He now sat down next to Tom's headstone and stared at it somberly. "What the hell am I supposed to do now?" he asked, bending over to pull the weeds that crept up the marker. He knew now that finding a prospective husband for Ginger was going to be next to impossible. How could he find a man for her when he wanted her himself?

How he wished Tom were here to tell him what to do. The absence of the old man was like a toothache, a dull pain that never quite went away. How he wished he could see Tom's eyes sparkling with pride, feel the warmth of the gnarled hand on his back, hear Tom's low voice saying, "You done good, boy."

But even if Tom could sit up and speak at this very moment, Judd knew those were not the words he'd say. Judd had let Tom down, left a promise unfulfilled. Tom had given Judd a home, accepted him without question into his life, and the only thing he'd asked of Judd, Judd couldn't do. The pain and guilt of that weighed heavily.

"Judd."

For a moment, he wondered if her voice had been conjured up out of his thoughts. Then he turned and saw her standing by the gate. She looked like an earthbound autumn deity, all reds and golds as the sunlight overhead stoked the fire of her hair and warmed the hues of her skin.

She wore an apricot-colored pair of shorts and a matching sleeveless blouse that only added to her beauty.

As Judd looked at her, his sense of betrayal to Tom was suddenly overwhelming, bringing tears to his eyes. He turned around, presenting her his back, hoping she would go away and let him wrestle with his problems alone. Instead he heard her footsteps whispering against the grass as she approached. He knew she was standing very close behind him because he was suddenly surrounded by her scent . . . the honey and clover freshness that he found so achingly provocative.

"Judd?" She sat down beside him and placed a hand on his arm. He closed his eyes, steeling himself against her.

"I came out here to be alone," he said, realizing his voice was harsh, wanting only for her to go away and leave him to sort out his thoughts, allow him the dignity of his own pain.

"Sorrow should be shared," Ginger said softly, remembering the night he'd allowed her to expend hers in his arms. But in whose arms had he grieved?

Judd started to protest, to tell her he was not grieving, but all of a sudden he was . . . the tight, emotional control he'd maintained since Tom's death shattered, leaving him alone with only cold, black anguish for the man who'd been like a father to him.

But he wasn't alone. Ginger was there, and as she saw his hands move up to hide his face, felt his broad shoulders begin to shake, she put her arms around him, drawing him into the shelter of her love.

He held himself stiffly at first, refusing to yield to her embrace. Slowly, almost imperceptibly, he relaxed, allowing himself a momentary weakness, giving in to the comfort she offered.

This was a side of Ginger that Judd had never seen . . . soft, nurturing . . . giving. He allowed himself to linger in her embrace, warmed by her nearness, drawing strength from venting the grief he'd kept trapped inside for too long.

As his emotion drained he felt renewed, invigorated. More than that, he found he was suddenly aware of other things, like the satiny feel of her skin beneath his hands, the curve of her neck against his face. If he moved his mouth just slightly, he could kiss the soft skin just below her jawline.

He pulled away from her, wanting to distance himself before he did something stupid. He was grateful that she didn't protest his moving away.

The reason Ginger had come to find Judd was forgotten for a moment as she studied his face, now firmly controlled, devoid of emotion.

In the brief time that he'd allowed her to hold him and share in his grieving, Ginger had faced reality. Judd had loved her grandfather deeply, and Tom had loved Judd as well. The love between the two men had little to do with her, and she had in no way been cheated because of it.

"I owe you an apology," she said, breaking the silence between them.

"For what?" he asked guardedly, not wanting to get into any kind of discussion with her. He still needed to sort out his feelings where she was concerned.

Ginger pulled her legs up against her chest and wrapped her arms around them, then rested her chin on her knees. "Ever since you arrived here years ago, I've been trying to devalue what you do around here, negate how important you were to this farm and Grandpa."

Judd shrugged. "It doesn't matter."

"But it does," she protested. "I think you were probably very important to Grandpa," she began, pausing to consider all the things that had swirled through her mind when she'd held Judd moments before. "When I came to Serenity to live, I was too young to consider that my losing my parents meant Grandpa and Grandma had lost their son and daughter-in-law. You probably helped ease that grief in Grandpa."

Ginger paused and took another deep breath. "I guess I was afraid that if I acknowledged how much Grandpa cared about you, it would somehow take away from how much he cared for me."

"Ginger." Judd smiled, a gentle one that made her heart thud more rapidly. "Nobody could take away from what Tom felt for you. He loved you as much as anyone could."

"And I left him, broke his heart." The anguish in her voice spoke of the last bit of leftover emotional baggage in her life.

"No—the other night when I said that, I was lying." Judd heaved a deep sigh. "At first he was upset, wondering what he'd done to make you leave. But when he found out that you'd gone to Loretta's, he was happy for you. He wanted so many things for you, Ginger. Things you couldn't have in the town of Gentry, here at Serenity. He had me read him your letters four and five times, reveling in the parts where you talked about the restaurants you'd eaten at, the theater productions you'd seen. He wanted all of that for you and he figured eventually, if you returned, it would be because you wanted to, not because you didn't know anything else."

"How I wanted to come back," Ginger sighed sadly. "But my pride was involved. I wanted Grandpa...and you...to beg me to come back. God," she laughed bitterly. "I was such a spoiled child."

"Ginger, your grandpa was functioning on pride, too. No matter how much he wanted you back here, he wouldn't ask. He felt it had to be your decision."

Ginger's voice caught on a sudden sob. "Stupid Taylor pride robbed me of the chance to be here at the end, tell him goodbye." She turned on him, her eyes full of the last of the anger that still ate at her. "Why did you wait three days to call me? Why did you rob me of the last chance to be a part of Grandpa?"

Judd touched her arm. "Ginger, I tried to contact you. Your Aunt Loretta told me you were upstate, staying with friends. I called, but I never could get an answer."

"Why didn't you keep calling until you reached me?"

Judd studied his fingernails, as if finding his cuticles immensely appealing. "I can't tell you why I didn't keep calling. I tried a few times, then people were coming at me, needing me to make decisions, take care of details. I can't tell you much about those three days immediately following your grandfather's death. I was in a fog, unable to believe he was gone."

There was something in his voice that spoke of quiet sorrow, deep despair. He'd been devastated by the loss of Tom, just as she had been, and she could now understand the fog of despair that had colored his world, made those three days slip by in a haze.

"Ginger, I can't give you back those days. We can't have another funeral because you missed the first. The only thing I can do is tell you I'm sorry."

This time it was his arms that enfolded her. And in his embrace was healing. The last little core of bitterness, the last fragment of anger and pain slowly ebbed away. Left behind was nothing to inhibit the love Ginger had growing in her heart for the man who had once been her sworn enemy. She pulled away from him. "Judd . . . about last night . . ."

In one swift movement he stood up, a curious tension in his stance. He stared down at her, drawn to the cinnamon warmth of her eyes. He knew a split-second decision had to be made. He had to admit to some feeling for her or he had to say something that would drive her away from him forever. "Yes, about last night." He pulled a hand over his chin, his gaze not meeting hers. "It's obvious there's something at work between us. I'm not sure what it is, and I definitely don't know what to do about it."

It's love, Ginger wanted to shout. But she didn't. She couldn't tell him what to feel, how to act. She wasn't sure how to handle the situation herself. It was all still too new. She simply looked at him, waiting for him to speak, loving him with her eyes.

"I suppose the best thing to do is to take this thing between us slowly, see where our feelings are leading," he finally said.

Ginger nodded, vaguely disappointed by his caution, but pleased that he was willing to go forward.

"Come on, let's go back to the house." He held out his hand to her.

Ginger took his hand, warmed by the way it enfolded hers so securely. It wasn't exactly what she'd wanted, but it was a beginning.

They didn't speak as they walked back to the house, nor did Judd release his hold on her hand.

Ginger felt as if they were embarking on something as new and wonderful as the signs of spring that surrounded them. She felt like a new blade of grass pushing up through thawed ground, or a flower opening itself to the warmth of the sun's loving rays. She was eager to travel the path of the unknown with Judd, knowing that no matter what the outcome was, he would always retain a piece of her heart, and she, his.

"I guess I'll finish up painting the back porch," Judd said as they approached the house.

"You need some help?"

Judd smiled at her, a sexy, half curve of his lips that made Ginger's blood thicken and pound. "I don't think painting is a job we do well together."

Ginger blushed, remembering the last time they had tried to work together, when the sparks of desire had flamed between them to the point of near combustion.

"Maybe you're right," she conceded. "I'll just go on inside and see if I can help Lisa with lunch."

He nodded and released his hold on her hand, and when he smiled at her, for a moment Ginger saw the emotions his lips had yet to speak.

She floated, rather than walked into the house, certain that it was just a matter of time before Judd could no longer deny the depth of his feelings for her. "Lisa," she called, wondering if the pregnant woman was here, or if she'd gone home to rest before beginning lunch preparations.

"In here." Lisa's voice was faint, coming from the kitchen.

She found Lisa sitting at the table. "Sit still. I'll get a cup of coffee and join you," Ginger said, moving to the cabinet to get a cup. "Are you feeling all right today?"

"Sure, but I'm having a baby."

Ginger laughed. "I should hope so, otherwise we need to discuss a drastic diet for you."

"No, I mean right now. I'm having the baby right now."

Ginger overshot her cup, spilling coffee across the counter as she whirled around to look at Lisa. It was then she realized the smile on Lisa's face was a grimace, and her hands were white knuckled and gripping the edge of the table.

"Oh, God, Lisa. How far apart are your pains?" Ginger slammed the coffeepot down and raced to Lisa's side.

"I don't know…four…maybe five minutes." Lisa blew a strand of damp hair away from her face and smiled crookedly, the pain apparently passing. "I guess this is it, huh?"

"I'll get Judd. We need to get you to the hospital."
Ginger ran to the back door. "Judd!" She spotted him
on his way to the barn. He stopped in his tracks,
turned and faced her. She cupped her hands to her
mouth, needing her voice to travel the distance. "Find
Ray. Lisa is having the baby."

Judd nodded, then as the words sank in, he took off
running in the direction of the chicken coops. Ginger
hurried back to Lisa, who was struggling to get to her
feet.

"Lisa, should you be getting up?"

Lisa smiled. "It's going to be difficult to get me to
the hospital if I don't get to the car."

"Okay, I'll help you into my car. I'll drive you to the
hospital and Ray can sit in the backseat with you."

It took only a minute or two to get Lisa settled in the
backseat. As she leaned back, another contraction
began. Ginger held Lisa's hands, allowing the older
woman to squeeze her fingers painfully until the contraction had ended.

At that moment Judd and Ray descended on the
car, the two men closely resembling a couple of Key-
stone Cops as they tripped over each other in an effort to see that Lisa was okay. Ray got into the back
seat with Lisa, and Judd jumped into the passenger
seat.

Ginger started the engine with a roar and flew down
the gravel driveway to the highway that would take
them to the hospital in Gentry.

Ginger concentrated on her driving, wanting to see
that mother-to-be and father got to their destination

quickly, but safely. In spite of her concentration, she was aware of Judd fidgeting nervously beside her. She smiled at him reassuringly.

"Don't worry, we'll get her there in time."

"Good. I've helped plenty in the birthing of cattle and horses, but a real baby..." His face blanched at the thought.

"Don't worry, Judd. I'm not about to let my son be born in the backseat of a car," Ray said. "Lisa and I have waited a long time for this. Surely this little fellow can wait until we get to the hospital."

"Oh, Ray, I can't believe it's really happening," Lisa said softly. "We're finally going to have our baby."

"And not a day will go by that this little critter doesn't know how loved he is...how loved his mother is."

Their words of intimacy and caring filled the car, making a lump in Ginger's throat. Could love get better than this? Creating and bringing a new life into the world? She looked over at Judd, wondering if he was as affected by all this as she was. He sat staring out the window, his expression not telling anything.

When they arrived at the hospital, there was a flurry of activity. Papers were filled out, questions answered, then Lisa was whisked away in a wheelchair and Ray, Judd and Ginger were sent to a room to wait...and wait...and wait.

Ray and Judd paced the floor, occasionally bumping into each other and smiling apologetically. It was

getting toward evening when Ginger convinced Judd
to go with her to the cafeteria and get them all something to eat.

"You think everything is okay?" Judd asked worriedly as he and Ginger got into the elevator that
would take them to the cafeteria. "It's taking so
long."

"I've heard that first babies almost always take a
long time." Ginger looked at him curiously, seeing the
lines of tension in his face. "Are you okay? I swear,
you seem as nervous as Ray."

"I just know how important this baby is to Lisa."
They stepped out of the elevator. "Lisa and I got real
close right after your grandpa's death. She helped me
through some rough times." He smiled at Ginger.
"She's sort of the sister I never had."

Ginger nodded. "Lisa's one of the most loving
women I've ever met. Their baby is going to be one
lucky little kid. It will be nice to have a baby around
Serenity."

"Yes, it will." For a moment he stared at her, and
she felt as if he was about to say something important, something wonderful. "Tuna fish or ham
salad?" he finally asked breaking the moment of anticipation.

They got the sandwiches and containers of coffee,
then hurried back to the waiting room, afraid to be
gone too long.

As Judd and Ginger ate, Ray continued to pace the
floor, occasionally taking a bite of the sandwich he
held. He finally threw himself into a chair and began

drumming his fingernails on the small table next to him.

Judd took up where Ray had left off, pacing back and forth, occasionally looking at his wristwatch. As he walked back and forth, he found himself wondering what it would be like if it was the woman he loved in there, giving birth to his child. The thought was appealing, more so than he'd ever dreamed. He'd always thought of himself as a solitary man, not really needing anyone. When he'd lost his mother, he'd vowed he would never love again, that loss was too painful. Tom had sneaked in beneath his defenses, and with his death, once again Judd had decided never to trust in love again. But Judd hadn't counted on Ginger coming back to his life with all her fire and vigor. The short, loving conversation between Ray and Lisa in the car had affected him more deeply than he'd thought and he now found himself reexamining his life.

He looked over to where Ginger sat, thumbing through an ancient magazine. God, she was so beautiful, so spirited. But it was more than her physical beauty that drew him to her like a ship to a beacon on a storm-tossed sea. She was passionate in her beliefs, fiercely loyal. When Ginger loved, it would probably be forever and with all her being. Rather than frightening him, this thought warmed him.

"Ray?" Doctor Weathers stepped into the waiting room, a broad grin on his face. "You are the father of a lusty, eight-pound baby boy. Both mother and baby are doing fine.''

The big, normally quiet man let out a whoop of joy that could be heard within a five-mile radius. Hugs abounded, then Ray was led in to see his wife and new son.

Once Ray and the doctor were gone, Judd and Ginger smiled at each other. ''What a day,'' Ginger said tremulously.

''A great day,'' Judd agreed, his eyes warm on her.

''Hey, Judd, Ginger...'' Ray stuck his head out the door. ''Come on in and see my boy.''

''Can we?'' Ginger asked tentatively, unsure about the hospital rules.

''Hell, I'm paying the bill, I guess I can invite in anyone I want,'' Ray boomed, motioning for them to follow him through the swinging door. They hurried after him.

The room he led them into was apparently the recovery room. Lisa was in bed, hooked up to a blood-pressure monitor, and in her arms, wrapped up in a blue blanket, was the baby.

''I wanted you to see him,'' Lisa said, smiling radiantly at her friends. She pulled aside the blanket, exposing a tuft of pale hair and the baby's sweet face. ''I want you to meet Thomas Edward.''

Ginger's breath caught in her throat as she realized Lisa and Ray had named the baby after her grandfather. It was the most wonderful kind of tribute to Tom.

She looked at Judd, wondering if he could possibly be feeling the same awe that she was experiencing. He was—it was there on his face as he stared down at the tiny newborn.

His gaze moved from the baby to Ginger, his eyes filled with the wonder of the miracle of birth. "Ginger, we need to talk." Without giving her a chance to respond, he grabbed her by the arm and pulled her out of the room.

Chapter Nine

Judd pulled Ginger back into the waiting room, frowning as he saw that several people now sat there. "We can't talk here," he muttered, pulling her on through the doorway that led outside.

Twilight was falling, the sun giving one final burst of orange and pink in the western sky before settling down for a night of sleep.

Judd took her over to a concrete bench that sat near the curb by the main road. He motioned for her to sit down, then leaned against the metal signpost that proclaimed the area a bus stop. For a long moment his gaze lingered on her face, studying her features with an intensity that made her blush.

"You're staring. Do I have mustard on my nose, or lettuce stuck on my teeth?" She looked at him curiously. He shook his head, not saying a word, continuing to look at her. "For goodness' sake, Judd. What are we doing out here? Did you pull me away from Lisa and Ray and the new baby just to stare at me as if I've suddenly grown an extra head?"

"No, I've come to a decision." Judd pushed himself away from the signpost and began to pace back and forth in front of the bench where she sat. "Right before Tom died, he asked me to do something for him." He stopped pacing and looked at her once again. "He asked me to find you a good husband."

"What?" Astonishment battled with outrage, the latter finally winning out, showing on her face. "That's the most ridiculous thing I've ever heard."

Judd shrugged. "Ridiculous or not, he asked and I agreed. I don't make my promises lightly."

"But... you... he..." she sputtered incoherently.

"I've tried," he continued, smoothly overriding her stuttering. "God knows, I've tried to think of a man who could put up with your horrendous temper, a man who wouldn't let you walk all over him. Somebody strong enough to tell you no when you need to be told. I've finally come to the conclusion that there's only one man in all the state of Kansas who could handle a woman like you."

"And just who is this model of macho strength and goodness that you've decided is right for me?" Her clipped tones attested to the anger that seethed just beneath the surface. Her eyes sparked like copper catching a fire's glow, and an answering fire ignited in the pit of Judd's stomach, letting him know that what he was about to say was intrinsically right.

"Me," he answered simply.

Ginger stared up at him, wondering briefly if this was all some sort of horrible, sadistic joke. But the light in his eyes was not humor, and no tell-tale grin lifted his lips upward. Instead there was a taut intensity to his physique, an unspoken longing in his eyes. This was no joke, and the realization of what he'd just said sucked her breath away. She stumbled to her feet, her heart expanding with joy. She walked up to him, standing so close they breathed the same particles of air, yet didn't physically touch.

"Why, Judd Bishop. Was that a proposal I just heard?"

He looked surprised, as if he hadn't considered where the conversation was leading until this very moment. Then, the left side of his mouth quirked up and the right side mirrored it, forming the sexy grin that had always made her think of languid caresses and throaty sighs.

"Yes . . . yes damn it, it is a proposal," he answered firmly.

"Then, my answer is yes," she replied, her eyes loving him. She smiled. "Shouldn't we kiss or something like that?"

"There won't be any 'something like that' until we're legally married. However, I'd say a kiss is definitely in order." With these words, he reached for her, enfolding her in an embrace that held the promise of the future. His lips took hers, communicating first tenderness, then passion.

Before, Judd had tried to hold himself in check, never forgetting the fact that it was Tom's granddaughter in his arms, stirring his lust. Now all inhibitions fell away as he registered the fact that it was his wife-to-be in his embrace. He drank of her honeyed sweetness, wanting to fall into the heat of her mouth. He anticipated the time when they could fully explore their passions, knowing Ginger would never be the kind of lover who merely took what was offered. She would demand, be an eager participant, meet his desire with a matched one of her own.

Ginger returned his kiss, her tongue battling his, thrust for thrust. All the energy and passion she'd ever brought to one of their arguments, she now directed into the kiss. As her lips moved against his, her commitment to him was complete.

"Hey, you two going to stand there all day doing mouth to mouth, or are you going to climb aboard?"

They sprang apart and looked in surprise at the bus that had eased to a halt next to where they stood. The door was open and the driver stared at them impatiently.

Judd motioned for the driver to move on, then he looked at Ginger, the flame of desire still burning in his dark eyes. "I have a feeling we'd better make this wedding soon. Otherwise I'm going to make love to you without the benefit of a legal commitment, and Tom's ghost will haunt me forever."

Ginger shivered, finding his desire for her wonderfully exciting. "I should be able to pull together a wedding ceremony in a month's time."

"A month?" Judd scowled and moved away from her. "I was thinking more in terms of next week."

"Next week?" This time Ginger frowned. "That's impossible, Judd. There are a million things to do." She moved against him again, twining her hands around his neck. "I intend for this wedding to be the only one of my life. I want everything perfect."

"Two weeks," Judd said firmly. "I don't want to begin our life together by fighting about the wedding, but I don't want to wait an entire month."

As she looked up into his smoldering eyes, feeling his hands moving slowly up and down her back, she didn't want to wait a month, either. "Okay," she agreed softly, "two weeks."

She suddenly realized that the weapons she'd always been able to use on a man to get her own way were ineffectual with Judd. He was strong enough to stand up for what he wanted, and when she was in his arms, she was weak enough to agree to anything.

As they walked back into the hospital, Ginger knew their marriage would be a good one. They'd learn to kiss away their differences, love away hostilities. Spiced with emotion, flavored with fire, their relationship would certainly never be dull.

If I don't have things all ready for the wedding in two weeks, we can set it up for three weeks, she rea-

soned to herself, thinking of all the preparations that
went into a marriage ceremony.

Judd looked at her, his eyes gleaming with the
knowledge of how her mind worked. "Two weeks,
Paprika. If things aren't ready in two weeks, I'll throw
you over my shoulder and bundle you off to a justice
of the peace."

Ginger laughed, knowing she'd been caught. She
smiled up at him. Yes, Judd was definitely man
enough for her.

"Don't ever ask me to get in that pen and feed those
god-awful creatures," Ginger said, watching Judd inside the chicken wire, scattering feed to the pecking,
squawking chickens.

"I can't figure out where you got such an irrational
fear of chickens," Judd replied, finishing the task at
hand and leaving the pen.

"I just hate them because they're so ugly."

"What are you going to do if we have ugly kids?
Are you going to hate them, too?" Judd's eyes shim-
mered with amusement as he walked up next to her.

"Of course not," she retorted. She turned to face
him and placed her hands on her hips. "Besides, what
makes you think we're going to have ugly kids?"

"They'll probably have your carrot-colored hair
and my oversized nose."

"Then get them jobs in the circus as clowns and my
hair is not carrot-colored." She grinned up at him,
looking at his nicely sculpted, perfectly proportioned

nose. "Although if our children inherit your nose, we can always get them nose jobs when they're old enough to be self-conscious," she teased.

His eyes sparked in reply, and he began to advance on her. "Take it back or I'm going to pick you up and toss you into the middle of the chicken pen."

Ginger backed up, a nervous giggle escaping her lips. "You wouldn't dare..."

"Oh, wouldn't I?"

His words broke the inertia that held her rooted to the spot, and with a wild shriek she turned to run.

She ran toward the house, her laughter making her breathless. He caught up with her, tackling her in the thick, overgrown grass. She lay beneath him, trying to catch her breath, unsure if it was difficult to breath because of the running or due to the fact that he lay on top of her, the length of his body trapping hers.

"You've been neglecting the mowing," she finally said, feeling the long grass tickling the sides of her face, trying to ignore the heat of his body, the firmness of him so molded to her.

"I'm just an employee around here," he replied, his breath on her face as provocative as a summer breeze on naked flesh. "I just do what I'm told."

"Starting next week you'll have to take a more active role in the running of this place. After all, it will be half yours."

He smiled at her, at the moment more taken with the way she looked than with their conversation. Her hair was a wild tousle of curls atop her head, and the grass whispered against her skin, the green emphasizing the creamy ivory of her flesh. Her eyes were clear, communicating only the language of love. The sunlight danced on her lashes, turning each one into starbursts of red and gold. She was beautiful, and in seven days, she would be his wife. It was a thought that made his breathing difficult. He only wished Tom was still here to give them his blessing. Would the old man be pleased? Would he think Judd was the right man for his granddaughter?

"Judd?" She looked up at him, seeing the frown that suddenly crossed his face. "Is everything all right?"

The frown was immediately replaced with a smile. "Everything is fine. I was just thinking that if I don't let you up now, I'll never get the rest of the chickens fed this afternoon. I'll just lie here in the grass and be content to while away the entire day looking at you."

Ginger smiled and reached up to caress his face with her fingertips. "That's just fine with me. I'll be glad to while away an afternoon with you anytime." Her smile suddenly changed to a look of horror. "What time is it?"

Judd sat up and looked at his wristwatch. "It's just after one o'clock."

Ginger sprang up from the grass, her hands immediately moving to smooth her riotous curls. "I've got to go. I've got an appointment in town at one-thirty. Mary Lynn Corbin and I are meeting to discuss the flowers.'' She blew him a kiss, then turned and ran toward the house.

Judd watched her go, not moving from his sitting position. He still couldn't quite believe the fact that he and Ginger were going to be married. He'd spent so much of his life pretending love didn't matter, that he had no space in his life for that particular emotion. In truth, he'd been afraid to believe in happy-ever-afters. His father…his mother…Tom…he'd lost in the love game so many times in the past.

But even though he'd tried to pretend he didn't need love, there had been a part of him that yearned for somebody, desired a commitment that would be so complete, so complex that it would fill his soul.

How strange…how wonderful that he would find it with the little minx who had been such a thorn in his side. How wonderful that Ginger had made him realize love was possible, and his dreams could come true. He'd stood in that hospital room, looking at Ray's and Lisa's new baby, and he'd realized he wanted the same thing. And he wanted it with Ginger.

He stood up and waved to her as she jumped into her car and tore off down the gravel road. Yes, dreams were coming true. No longer would Serenity be split. Starting next Saturday, Serenity would be shared. Serenity, yes, that's what he would have with Ginger, whether it be here on the farm that was its namesake or elsewhere.

With a small shake of his head, wondering at his fanciful thoughts, he headed back for the work that awaited him at the pens.

"I don't want roses," Ginger explained to Mary Lynn. "It's just going to be a very small ceremony, and roses seem pretentious."

"Honey, weddings are supposed to be pretentious," Mary Lynn Corbin protested, her chubby hands working to arrange a mixture of spring flowers in a ceramic cow-shaped vase. "How about lilacs? They're always nice for a spring wedding, and they smell so pretty." Mary Lynn frowned. "Oh, but the purple might clash, you know, you being a redhead and all." She continued before Ginger could respond. "Daisies, now they'd be real nice. Of course Mrs. Greenworth over at the high school, she's allergic to daisies. So if she's invited, you'd better go with something else."

"Actually, she's not invited. As I said before, it's a very small ceremony, only about twenty guests." Ginger sighed and looked at her watch. She'd been in the flower shop nearly a half hour, and all she'd managed to get accomplished was to develop a headache from the sweet, cloying floral scents, and hear all the gossip that had traveled the town's rumor mill in the past twenty-four hours. Mary Lynn had a gift with flowers, but she had a bigger talent for gossip.

"Everybody sure was surprised to hear about you and Judd deciding to tie the knot. The whole town's been buzzing with the news ever since you and Judd showed up at the jewelry store yesterday. Picked out your rings, did you?"

Ginger nodded, a smile playing on her face as she remembered the occasion and the gold wedding bands that now rested in velvet-lined boxes back at the farm. "Now, about the flowers, I think daisies will be fine."

Mary Lynn finished up her cow arrangement and picked up an order pad. "So, I'll do a bridal bouquet with daisies and baby's breath, and a matching boutonniere for that handsome man you're going to marry."

That handsome man you're going to marry. Those words carried Ginger out of the flower shop with a happy smile once her business was completed. There were moments when Ginger still couldn't believe that in less than seven days, she would be Ginger Bishop. She'd begun to wonder lately if when she'd packed her bags and left the farm so long ago, it wasn't something more than jealousy for Judd that had made her run. She could now remember moments when their hands would touch across the kitchen table and her breath would suddenly catch in her throat and warmth would crawl up her neck and cover her face. She'd thought at the time it was hatred for him, anger at the enviable position he'd attained in her grandfather's affections. At seventeen years old, she'd been too emotionally immature to recognize that there was more at work, that her emotions where Judd was concerned were not so easy to discern as simple hatred.

Once outside the flower shop, Ginger headed for the boutique where she had bought her wedding dress the afternoon before. She had promised the seamstress at the shop that she'd be in this afternoon to have her dress hemmed.

A little bell tinkled as she pushed open the door of the boutique. Mrs. O'Brian, the seamstress, met her just inside the doorway. "Ah, there she is . . . the prettiest bride the town of Gentry will ever see."

Ginger laughed. "I won't be the prettiest if I trip over my skirt on the way down the aisle."

"We're going to fix that right now. You just get on back in that dressing room and pull the dress on, then I'll make you look like a walking dream." The bird-thin woman ushered Ginger into the back room, where her dress hung waiting for her.

It took her only minutes to get it on. Although the wedding was to be small, Ginger's wedding gown would have been perfectly appropriate for a ceremony of two hundred people. A floor-length white silk, it emphasized Ginger's tiny waist, and the off-the-shoulders neckline bared her creamy shoulders.

Once she had the dress on, Ginger stared at her reflection in the dressing room mirror. It looked beautiful . . . she looked beautiful. She ran her hands down the slippery silk fabric of the skirt, her vision blurring with a sudden veil of tears. "Oh, Grandpa," she breathed. How she wished he could be here with her.

She'd always dreamed that he would be the one giving her away, smiling at her as he handed her ceremoniously to the man who would be her husband. Would he be happy that she was marrying Judd? Somehow she thought so. He'd loved Judd. She knew all her grandfather had ever wanted for her was happiness, and wasn't that what Judd was offering her? A lifetime of love and happiness?

She swiped at the tears with the backs of her hands. The one thing Tom would not want was for her wedding day to be stained with tears for him. "Mrs. O'Brian, I'm ready," she called out. While she waited for the woman to join her in the dressing room, Ginger smiled at her reflection. No more tears . . . she saw only a woman radiantly smiling, a woman with love in her eyes.

By the time the dress had been hemmed and Ginger left the boutique, she was exhausted. Her stomach grumbled, reminding her that she had skipped lunch. She was also excited. The alterations on the dress had been the last of the details for the wedding. Everything was ready, all systems go for her to become Mrs. Judd Bishop.

She paused across the street from the café that Amanda Withers owned, thinking of the heavenly chocolate meringue pies the woman baked. A piece of pie would revive her batteries. There was nothing like rich chocolate to renew her energy level. Still she hesitated. She hadn't seen Amanda since the night of the dance, and she had to admit there was a little bit of leftover jealousy in her heart as she thought of all the evenings Judd had spent with the blond woman. But Ginger's grumbling stomach made the decision for her. Besides, Ginger thought, Gentry was a small town, she couldn't spend the rest of her life avoiding Amanda Withers.

Amanda was inside, standing behind the register. Ginger smiled a greeting, then took a seat at one of the empty booths. There were only two other people inside, an older couple enjoying a quiet meal.

The waitress, a buxom brunette, stuck her nail file into her apron pocket and sauntered over to where Ginger sat.

"A piece of chocolate pie and a cup of coffee," Ginger said pleasantly, aware of the cool glares Amanda was sending her way. Apparently she had heard of Ginger's and Judd's wedding plans, and she was not pleased.

The waitress nodded and departed, returning in minutes with Ginger's order.

Ginger had eaten half the piece of pie when she realized Amanda and the waitress were talking loudly enough for her to hear, and Ginger was the subject of their conversation.

"Rather a hurry-up affair if you ask me. I heard they're only inviting a few people. Makes you wonder what the real story is." Amanda arched a perfectly penciled eyebrow.

Ginger pretended not to notice, but again she found herself wondering what the relationship between Judd and Amanda had been. Amanda definitely sounded like a woman scorned. Deciding not to give Amanda the satisfaction of a reaction, Ginger directed her attention to the pie in front of her, savoring each and every rich bite.

"You know, Judd loves that farm. He worked like a dog around that place. He had big dreams, he told me about them often. He'd hoped Tom would remember that, when it came to the will. He was so disappointed when he wasn't left a piece of Serenity." Amanda's volume had risen, making it impossible for Ginger to ignore. "Oh, well." Amanda's laugh tinkled irritatingly. "I guess Judd wins, anyway. If you can't inherit it . . . marry it."

The bite of pie in Ginger's mouth went down sourly, awash with the acidity of Amanda's words.

She's just jealous, Ginger reasoned, trying to remain calm, desperately fighting down a feeling of cold despair. Ignore her, she told herself. But she couldn't.

She pushed the half-eaten pie away, knowing if she took another bite she'd choke on it. She got up from the booth, finding the warmth of the café and the mixture of cooking odors stifling. She needed to think.

"Why, Ginger, I see you only ate half your pie," Amanda said as Ginger approached the cash register. "I hope you're feeling all right?" Amanda's tone was sweet and solicitous, her facial expression pleasantly innocent.

"I'm feeling wonderful, Amanda." Ginger returned the blonde's smile and handed her the money to pay her bill. "I only ate half the pie because, frankly, dear, it just wasn't quite up to par." Ginger felt a flare of satisfaction as Amanda frowned. She knew how proud Amanda was of her baking skills. Amanda's pies were known around three counties and always took first prize at the state fair. Ginger leaned forward conspiratorially as she accepted her change and continued in a voice loud enough for the other two patrons to hear. "Actually, it had a horrendous aftertaste, and I do believe I saw a cockroach skitter across the top of my table as I sat down." Raising an eyebrow, Ginger exited the café, sure that everyone in town would soon know that Amanda's establishment had bugs.

Ginger maintained her calm exterior until she got into the car. It wasn't until she began the drive back toward the farm that Amanda's words came back to haunt her. *If you can't inherit it, marry it.* The hateful words twirled around and around in her head, making her wonder exactly what had prompted the sudden proposal of marriage from Judd. Had it been love for her that had made him decide he couldn't live without her, or had it been his love for Serenity? He'd certainly never tried to hide his feelings for the land. His proposal to her had come out of nowhere. What had prompted it? She needed to find out before the wedding.

As a plan began to formulate in her mind, she turned the car around, heading back into town. There was one last bit of business she had to take care of, a plan that would let her know for sure if Judd's love for her was true.

Chapter Ten

It was after dark when Ginger finally pulled her car into the garage. For a long moment she sat unmoving, clutching her purse, which held the papers Mr. Roberts, the lawyer, had drawn up for her.

You don't have to do this, she told herself. You can marry Judd on Saturday and remain blissfully ignorant as to the forces that drove him to marry you. And yet, even as she considered this, she knew she could never do it. She couldn't go into a marriage not knowing whether she was loved. She had to know what was more important to Judd, her or the farm.

She got out of the car and closed the garage door, walking hesitantly toward the porch, dreading the conversation to come.

She stood at the wooden railing, looking out over the land before her. The full moon rising gave the landscape a soft illumination, the light playing in the boughs of the ancient oak trees and dancing on the waters of the distant pond.

She loved this place with a passion that had been passed down through the generations. She would fight anyone to keep it, attack anyone who tried to take it. She would sacrifice whatever was necessary to hang on to it. She only hoped she didn't have to make the ultimate sacrifice of love.

The front door creaked open. Ginger looked around to see Judd step out on the front porch. She returned her attention to the moonlit fields in the distance.

"Where have you been? I was beginning to really get worried." His voice was low as he came to stand behind her, wrapping his arms around her and gently pulling her toward him.

Ginger leaned against him and closed her eyes, wishing his embrace was enough to erase her doubts, take away her fears. But it was not. Still, she remained in his arms, reluctant to move away from the enveloping warmth of his body so close to hers.

"It's beautiful out here, isn't it?" His breath was warm against her ear.

"Yes, it is." She moved out of his embrace, his words reminding her of the dilemma that weighed heavily on her heart.

"I had to stop by Mr. Roberts's office. I had some business to take care of," she said, gazing at him, noticing how the moonlight loved his features. The pale glow turned his gray eyes to a pale silver and emphasized the clean-cut facial lines. Her love for him pressed thickly in her chest, battling with the doubts that whirled around in her head.

"Why? Is there some sort of legal problem concerning Serenity?" Judd's dark eyebrows shot up quizzically.

Ginger shivered suddenly, despite the warmth of the night air. "Let's go inside," she suggested, moving to go into the house.

She led him into the kitchen, somehow needing the harsh glare of the overhead lights to face what was to come. "Sit down," she said, motioning for him to sit at the table as she drew the legal documents out of her purse.

Judd smiled at her indulgently as she handed him the paperwork. "You're certainly being mysterious. What is this?"

"Just read. It's pretty self-explanatory," she replied, knowing very well she wasn't being mysterious. She was being a coward by just shoving the papers in his face instead of telling him what she wanted from him.

She watched him anxiously as he read, hoping, praying that he would laugh at her silliness, sign the papers and relieve her fears.

She knew the exact moment the meaning of the words sank into his consciousness. His smile fell from his face, and when he looked up at her his eyes had changed to the metal-gray shade that always warned of stormy seas ahead.

"Is this some kind of a joke?" he asked, slamming the papers down on the top of the table. "This is a prenuptial agreement."

Ginger nodded, seeing the way his jaw clenched, the angry set of his shoulders. She'd known he would be upset, but hadn't expected the rage she saw simmering just beneath the surface. "Judd, a lot of people today sign prenuptial agreements."

"So in other words, you really don't expect our marriage to last and want to protect your interests."

"It's a smart business move," Ginger hedged.

"But we're not talking business, we're talking about us." He shoved back his chair and stood up, his inner turmoil still evident in the rigidity of his body as he began to approach her.

"It's not that big a deal." Ginger felt a nervous giggle bubbling up her throat, but she made a conscious effort to swallow it, knowing it would only make things worse. "All it says is that if anything happens between us, Serenity remains mine."

He'd come to stand directly before her, his face a vivid reflection of his inner turmoil. "Ginger, please . . . don't ask me to sign those papers."

"I have to," she answered, her voice a mere whisper of emotion. "If you love me, you'll sign."

Judd swore and stepped back from her. "Don't you understand? This has nothing to do with love. It has everything to do with trust. And it's obvious you don't

trust me." He swore again, as if having no control over
the curses that slid out of his mouth. He stared at her
for a long moment, then with a sigh of frustration, he
turned and headed for the back door.

"Judd?"

He stopped with his hand on the doorknob, his back
to her, his body taut with anger.

"If you don't sign the papers, then I'm calling off
the wedding." They were the most difficult words
Ginger had ever spoken. She stared at his broad back,
willing him to turn around, wanting him to rush to
her, agree to sign anything for her.

The seconds clicked by and he didn't move. Then
his shoulders sagged slightly. "So be it." He disappeared out the door.

Judd walked with long, purposeful strides, unsure
of his destination, but hoping the physical activity
would ease the strange ache in the pit of his stomach,
the fullness in his chest.

There was a sense of unreality about the whole
thing. He felt like a character in a tabloid report, a
nobody trying to marry a wealthy movie star. *A prenuptial agreement*...the words cut through his pride,
making him feel battered and bruised. Was she really
so unsure of his motives in marrying her? Was she really so suspicious of his love?

He found himself by the cemetery, the full moon illuminating the area in a ghostly light. He paused at the
gate, then changed his mind and went to sit beneath a
nearby weeping willow tree.

He'd thought he'd plummeted to the depths of despair when Tom had died, but that didn't even begin to measure up to the cold agony that gripped him now.

It was his own fault, really. He'd allowed himself to hope. He'd dropped his defenses and had begun to believe that all his dreams for love, for family... were possible. The dreams of a fool, that's all they had been.

Serenity... what a joke. Ginger's ancestors should have named the place Hell's Little Acres.

He rubbed his hands over his eyes, silently asking Tom's forgiveness. He wasn't going to fulfill his promise to the old man. He wasn't even going to try anymore. In truth, Judd didn't know what he was going to do now.

Happy is the bride that the sun shines on. Ginger thought of the little saying as she got out of bed and padded to her window.

It was Saturday, the morning of what should have been her wedding day. But there would be no wedding, and there was no sun, only a sky of low-hanging gray clouds. The dismal skies seemed to reflect Ginger's mood for the past several days.

She'd cried until she wondered if it was possible she'd completely dehydrate herself. She'd canceled all the wedding arrangements and moved through a haze of despair.

But this morning, the tears were long gone, the gray haze had lifted, and her friend, anger, had returned.

She wrapped this new emotion around her like a long-lost favorite coat, finding strength and self-righteousness as she gazed out the window at the clouds that were the exact shade of Judd's eyes.

Judd... For the last couple of days they had studiously avoided each other, rarely being in the same room at the same time.

As she dressed, she thought of the man she had almost married. Thank God she had discovered what he was up to before actually going through with the wedding. All he wanted was Serenity. That was all he'd ever wanted. Now, if she could just stop loving him, everything would be back to normal.

Finished dressing, she went downstairs and into the kitchen. Judd wasn't in the room, but there was evidence that he'd been there recently. A fresh pot of coffee had been made, and a pot of chili simmered on the stove, its pungent odor filling the kitchen. Since the birth of the baby, Judd and Ginger had been on their own, as Lisa had taken some time off to devote to her infant.

Ginger poured herself a cup of coffee and frowned at the chili. Judd knew she hated it. She'd never been able to tolerate the dish. He'd probably made it on purpose because he knew she hated the spicy stuff.

She took her coffee and sat down at the kitchen table, gathering her shield of anger as Judd walked into the room.

"I need to talk to you," he said without preamble, stalking over to the pot and pouring himself a cup of coffee.

"Well, maybe I don't want to talk to you," she returned coolly.

He slammed his cup down on the table, the liquid sloshing out over the top and onto the tablecloth. "I need to talk to you about farm business. Damn it, Ginger, as long as I'm going to remain working here, you're going to have to talk to me."

"If you don't like the working conditions here, you can always leave." She looked at him defiantly.

Judd stared back at her, finding it difficult to believe that after all the hurt, all the pain, he still wanted her more than he'd ever wanted anyone. "Oh, you'd like that, wouldn't you. I wouldn't be surprised if that was your motive for that ridiculous prenuptial agreement. You wanted to make me angry enough that I would leave."

"It wasn't ridiculous," she returned. "It certainly proved to me what was important to you."

For a moment they stared at each other, their anger a vivid, living thing in the air between them. "You always were spoiled. You always had to have things your own way." Judd's adrenaline raced through him as it hadn't done in days.

"Oh, look who's talking," Ginger said snorting.

He glared at her in frustration, not knowing if he wanted to punish her by throttling her, or by kissing her until she was too weak to move. "Are you going to talk to me or not?" he asked tersely.

Ginger returned his glare. "Not. I'm not in the mood to discuss business right now. I'd like to enjoy my coffee in peace, preferably in my own company." She drained her cup and got up to pour herself more coffee.

"I can't run this farm based on your moods. As usual you're just being perverse."

"I'll show you perverse," she exclaimed, the control she'd been maintaining snapped, and she raised the stoneware cup above her head. Before she could release it, Judd was across the room and captured her arm in a tight grip.

"That temper of yours is going to get you in over your head someday. You're crazy, but I must have been out of my mind to ever consider marrying you. A man doesn't want a steady diet of Cayenne pepper." With these words he slammed out the door.

The moment the door closed, Ginger released the cup. Like a missile, it hit the wood of the door and shattered. She knew it was a childish act, but her frustration was too great to control.

"Ohhh..." Ginger looked around, needing to further vent her anger.

Cayenne pepper...she paced around the room, her rage coursing hotly through her. She'd give him cayenne pepper, she thought, rummaging around in the spice cabinet. Spying the tin, she opened it and dumped the hot spice into the pot of chili that was bubbling on the stove.

Later that evening Ginger sat at the table, trying to eat a sandwich. She really wasn't hungry, but she hadn't eaten all day and knew she needed to put something in her stomach.

She was restless, feeling like a time bomb ticking down to detonation. The weather outside wasn't helping matters any. There was an electrical force in the air, a static crackling as the clouds overhead darkened and thickened.

Another storm was threatening, and as much as Ginger hated thunder and lightning, she was anticipating the storm, hoping it would not only relieve the oppression in the air, but also blow out some of her own tension.

She'd spent the day wandering around the farm, avoiding Judd and thoughts of him. She'd visited Lisa, grateful that the woman asked nothing about the canceled wedding plans. Ginger's visit there was brief because she found being with Lisa and the newborn baby almost physically painful, reminding Ginger of all she might have had, but now wouldn't.

She looked up as Judd entered the kitchen. He studiously ignored her as he got a bowl out of the cabinet and began to ladle up his chili.

Ginger tried to hide her pleasure as she thought of the spice she'd added to his meal. She hoped the cayenne pepper burned his tongue right out of his head.

He grabbed a handful of saltine crackers, then joined her at the table, sitting directly across from her.

"What's up your sleeve?" he asked, looking at her suspiciously.

"What do you mean?" She feigned innocence, hoping his first bite caused steam to blow out his ears and flames to shoot out of his mouth.

"You look guilty as hell," he grumbled, breaking up several crackers and stirring them around. He then picked up his spoon and took a big, healthy bite. "Hmm, best chili I've ever made."

His words made Ginger's anticipation deflate like a leftover party balloon. She got up from the table and left the kitchen, heading up to her bedroom where she could be alone with her thoughts.

The minute she left the room, Judd shoved back from the table and raced to the refrigerator. He grabbed the water jug and drank deeply, trying to ease the burning that brought tears to his eyes. He took the cold water over to the sink and rinsed his mouth out several times. The little minx. He'd known by her expression as she'd sat across from him that she'd been up to some mischief. It had been all he could do to swallow that first bite and smile at her nonchalantly. He wasn't about to give her any satisfaction for her little trick.

There was no way he could eat the chili, but it didn't matter. He wasn't hungry, anyway. The brewing storm was causing a disquiet in him, a restlessness that seemed to have no definite source.

Not a minute of this day had passed that he hadn't been aware that today should have been his wedding day. Tonight should have been the night he finally held Ginger in his arms, fulfilled the passion that thus far had been just a promise between them.

Why in the hell had she wanted him to sign that damned prenuptial agreement? Hadn't she realized how much it would hurt, how the agreement would stand between them and eventually destroy their marriage? By asking him to sign it she had demeaned his love for her, questioned his honor.

As thunder rumbled overhead, he decided to go back out to the barn. He'd begun cleaning the large outbuilding that afternoon. Maybe a couple more hours of physical exertion would make him too exhausted to think, too tired to dream about Ginger and what might have been.

Ginger stood next to her window, watching nature's display of temper. Like a child in the middle of a tantrum, Mother Nature grumbled her dissent and threw lightning like a child throws toys.

Night had fallen as quickly as somebody pulling down a shade over a window. Other than the lightning that sizzled in the skies, the darkness was complete.

She moved away from the window, trying to fight down the sense of panic that always assailed her during one of these storms. A ray of pain swept through her as she remembered that during the last weather tempest she'd found comfort and relief in Judd's strong arms. There would be no comfort there now. In fact, he was probably sitting downstairs just waiting for her to run to him in a panic. Well, it wasn't going to happen. If she had to crawl beneath her bed with all the dust bunnies to escape the storm, it was better than seeking Judd's company.

She jumped and screamed involuntarily as there was a loud crash and her bedroom lit up with a flash so brilliant she was momentarily blinded.

When her eyes had readjusted, she went back to the window. It had sounded like the lightning had struck something dangerously close. She looked out, seeing nothing untoward. Lightning once again flared and when the brief illumination died, Ginger saw a flicker of red-gold flame dancing on the roof of one of the distant chicken coops. Fire... the word evoked terror.

"Judd... the coops are on fire," she yelled, nearly stumbling down the stairs. She ran into the kitchen, but he wasn't there. She raced back up the stairs to his bedroom, but he wasn't there, either. Dear God, where was he?

She ran back downstairs and to the back door. The flames were higher now, brighter, and in them Ginger saw all of Judd's hopes, all his dreams for the future of Serenity going up in smoke. No matter what had transpired between the two of them, no matter what hurt still lay in her heart, she couldn't just stand here and watch Judd's dreams go up in flames. Without another thought, driven only by the love that still burned in her heart, Ginger ran out into the storm.

The wind viciously tore at her, making her advance to the coops difficult. Thunder shook the earth and lightning seemed to be chasing her as she ran.

As she got closer, she realized only one of the coops was on fire. The roof of the coop that held the chickens ready for market was flaming in two different places, and already the flames had advanced down the side of the building near the door. Even above the din of the storm she could hear the frantic squawking of the birds from inside. Black smoke was billowing, making Ginger cough as she advanced closer. She had to do something. It wouldn't take long for all the chickens to die from carbon monoxide poisoning. She had to get close enough to open the door and let the chickens escape.

She covered her face with one arm and ran toward the door, the heat of the blaze burning her flesh. Soot swirled in the air, settling on her hair, making her choke. The door handle was hot, but she managed to unlatch it and pull it open. She stepped back, waiting for the chickens to come flying out. Only two rushed out, flapping their wings and voicing their fear. Ginger waited for more to follow. Nothing happened. She could still hear the noise of hysteria coming from inside.

Then she remembered why she hated chickens so much. It wasn't just that they were ugly and noisy and dirty... it was because they were dumber than rocks.

They were too stupid to run to the open door to escape their death. She was going to have to go into the coop and herd them out.

After only a moment's hesitation, seeing the smoke that billowed out from within, Ginger stripped off her T-shirt, held it over her mouth and nose, then plunged into the smoke-filled inferno.

Judd sighed heavily and swiped at his forehead with the back of his arm. He looked around in satisfaction. The barn was cleaner than it had been in years.

He needed to go back into the house, find Ginger. She was probably cowering someplace, trying to hide from the sounds of the storm that raged outside. Even though he was still angry with her, still hurt, he knew she would need his support to get through the storm. And he couldn't deny her that comfort. No matter how things stood between them, he didn't want her facing her demons alone.

He stepped outside the barn, feeling the first raindrops splattering his head, blowing into his face. He'd begun to run toward the house when he glanced toward the coops and saw the orange glow. Good God, the coops were on fire. He changed directions, running down the sloping hill that led to the area, his heart beating frantically in his chest.

As he got closer he saw that chickens were running loose everywhere. How had they gotten out? By the look of the fire consuming the building, they should have been barbecued. As he contemplated this, he saw chickens scattering out the opened door of the coop, and closely behind the chickens came a half-naked Ginger, her hair soot darkened as she waved her hand over her head, cursing and screaming. Judd's heart crawled up in his throat as he ran to her.

"Ginger...what in the hell are you doing?" he yelled, grabbing her and pulling her away from the burning building, quickly checking to make sure she was all right.

"I'm trying to save your damned, dumb chickens," she yelled back, swiping at her teary, sooty face with the back of her hand.

At that moment the rain began in earnest. "Come on," he said, pulling her toward the barn.

"But what about the fire?"

"Hopefully the rain will put it out," he answered.

They ran for the barn, the rain soaking them to the skin by the time they reached the safety of cover.

Inside the weathered old building, Ginger collapsed on a clean bed of hay. Judd found an old work shirt and wordlessly handed it to her, then joined her on the hay. Ginger slipped into the shirt. It smelled of Judd, the clean, alfalfa and sunshine odor that belonged to him alone.

"We can rebuild the coop. Most of the chickens got out," Ginger said after she'd caught her breath.

Judd shook his head. "It will be your decision," he said. He ran a hand through his hair and looked at her. With her hair nearly black and her face sooty and streaked, she looked more beautiful to him than ever, and he realized what he had to do. There was no way he could remain here at Serenity, watching her, loving her, but knowing he wasn't ever going to have her. Serenity had been important to him, but he suddenly realized if he couldn't have Ginger, the farm no longer seemed important. "I'm leaving, Ginger."

His voice was so low, his words so soft, for a moment she wondered if she'd misunderstood. "What?"

He looked away, not meeting her gaze. "You finally get what you want. I'll be gone by the end of the week and Serenity will be all yours."

Ginger stared at him, waiting to feel the elation she'd always assumed she'd feel if he ever left Serenity, but there was no elation. Only a deep desolation that made tears burn at her eyes. "No," she whispered involuntarily.

She suddenly realized that where a week ago she had been willing to sacrifice her love for Judd to hold on to Serenity, she now knew she was willing to sacrifice the farm for love. And she did love Judd, with every fiber of her being, every breath of her body.

What she had begun to realize was that Serenity was just a piece of land. What had made it home was Tom and Judd. Tom was gone forever, but Judd, he was here, and she needed him. It had been stupid Taylor pride that had kept her from her grandfather. She wasn't going to allow that pride to interfere twice in her lifetime.

"You can't leave," she said, her voice strong and firm.

"Why not?" He looked at her in surprise. The last thing he had expected from her was an objection concerning his leaving.

"You promised Grandpa you'd see me married to a good man, and you told me you don't give your promises lightly." She moved closer to him. "I don't care about that stupid prenuptial agreement. It was just my own insecurities wanting it signed. You don't have to sign it. But you do have to marry me. You know you're the only man in these parts who's man enough for me." She smiled at him impishly. "And if you marry me you're doing yourself a favor. You're too pigheaded and stubborn, ill-tempered and mean for any other woman to put up with. I'm the only one around these parts who's woman enough for you."

Judd stared at her for a long moment, the love shining from her eyes washing over him, healing all wounds, promising joy. "Ginger, I'll sign whatever you want me to sign. This place doesn't mean anything to me unless I can share my life with you. Before...when you asked me to sign it, I felt like you were doubting me...doubting my love. But I don't care anymore. I want you on any terms."

In a heartbeat they were in each other's arms, their lips making promises that would be fulfilled later.

"How fast can you get a wedding party together?" Judd asked when their lips parted momentarily.

"First thing tomorrow morning?" she answered breathlessly. He nodded his agreement, then claimed her lips again.

As Judd held her, all of the doubts that had assailed Ginger earlier ebbed away, leaving her only with the shining knowledge that she was loved by him. She knew theirs would be a stormy relationship, but always beneath the storm would be a shelter of love.

"I think the rain has stopped," Judd said as his lips left hers once again. "Maybe we should head back to the house."

She nodded. Together they got up and stepped outside into the darkness. The rain had stopped, and the thunder was a distant rumble. The storm had passed, as they always would. The coop was still smoldering, but the flames were out, the rain had done a good job. Judd placed his arm around her shoulders, and they walked toward the house.

"I just want you to know that I do owe you one," Judd said as they walked in the back door.

"For what?" She looked at him curiously.

Judd grinned, the spark in his gray eyes promising revenge. "For whatever it was you did to my chili."

Ginger giggled. "Let's just hope I'm not too hot for you to handle."

"Oh, I think I'll manage somehow." He pulled her into his arms, and Ginger melted against him. As he gazed down at her, his eyes filled with love, Ginger knew she had found her real Serenity, and it was here in his arms.

Epilogue

"Come on, Judd. Everything is going to get cold," Ginger yelled up the stairs. She flew back into the living room to make sure her surprise was all ready. A checkered tablecloth lay neatly in the middle of the floor. In the center of the tablecloth was an ice bucket holding a bottle of chilling wine. The picnic basket was nearby, packed with the goodies Ginger had spent the day cooking. Yes, everything was ready.

She went back to the bottom of the stairs. "Judd Bishop, get your buns down here or dinner is going to be ruined."

"Okay, okay, keep your britches on," Judd said, coming out of the bathroom dressed in clean jeans and shirt, his hair still damp from his shower.

"Now that's something I haven't heard from you before," Ginger exclaimed with a grin.

Judd laughed as he joined her at the bottom of the stairs. He kissed the end of her nose and put his arm around her. "Now, what's this surprise you've been so anxious about?"

Ginger led him into the living room. "Ta da."

"What's this? A picnic?"

"A very special one," she said, wrapping her arms around his neck. "It's a happy-one-week anniversary picnic."

"How come an indoor picnic, why not outside?"

"Because if we were outside, I couldn't do this." She pulled his head down so she could kiss him. Then, with an impish grin she stepped back, her eyes gleaming with the red fires he'd come to anticipate. "And if we were outside, I couldn't wear this." She unbuttoned her dress and stepped out of it, exposing a pale green teddy that revealed more than it hid of her creamy flesh and sexy curves.

"Hmm," Judd pulled her back into his arms, his lips finding the sensitive skin just behind her ear. "I think I'm going to love indoor picnics."

"Wait," Ginger said breathlessly, trying to halt his ear-nibbling before she lost all rational thought. "We have food."

"Who needs food?" he murmured, continuing his exploration of her tender neck.

"Judd, I cooked all day. If we don't eat now, everything will be cold."

"Okay." He released her reluctantly and sat down on the floor. As he watched, she got out the food, arranging everything on plates. The green teddy whispered against her skin, allowing him teasing glimpses of femininity, and he wondered if there would ever come a time when the mere thought of her wouldn't evoke desire.

The past week of married life had been beyond Judd's wildest expectations. He worked the farm every day, rebuilding the coop that had burned, then reached new heights of splendor in Ginger's arms each night.

"Hmm, looks good," he said as she handed him a plate filled with fried chicken, baked beans, potato salad and slices of cheddar cheese. He eyed the chicken dubiously. "This isn't..."

Ginger laughed. "No, I got it from the grocery store yesterday."

They had just begun to eat when there was a knock on the door.

"I'll get it," Ginger jumped up.

Judd reached out and grabbed her hand. "Not dressed like that. That's a view reserved only for me."

As she grabbed her dress and ran upstairs, Judd answered the door, surprised to see the lawyer, Mr. Roberts, standing there.

"Mr. Bishop," the bespectacled man shook Judd's hand. "I saw in the paper the other day the announcement that you and Miss Taylor had married. Congratulations."

"Thanks." Judd smiled curiously, wondering why the man would make a trip from town to the farm just to extend his congratulations.

Mr. Roberts drew an envelope out of his breast pocket. "Uh, I know this is a little irregular, but when Tom made out his will, he also left me this envelope. I was to give it to you if you and Miss Taylor married."

Judd took the envelope, a frown on his forehead. "And what were you supposed to do if we didn't marry?"

"I was told in that case to throw it away."

"Would you like to come in, have a cup of coffee or something?" Judd asked, grateful when the man shook his head.

"No, I was on my way to another appointment and just wanted to see that you got that. Again, congratulations on your recent marriage."

Judd thanked the man, then closed the door, his curiosity piqued as he fingered the plain, white envelope. He opened it up and withdrew the sheet of paper inside. Unfolding it and reading it, Judd felt a mist of tears veiling his eyes.

"Judd?" Ginger came to stand next to him, her concern evident. "I heard what Mr. Roberts said. What is it? Is something wrong?"

"No, everything is wonderfully all right." He handed her the piece of paper. Written on it in Tom's strong, bold strokes were four words... "You done good, boy."

* * * * *

Silhouette
ROMANCE™

COMING NEXT MONTH

#886   A CHANGED MAN—Karen Leabo   *Written in the Stars*
Conservative Virgo man Stephen Whitfield was too uptight for
impulsive Sagittarius Jill Ballantine. But Jill sensed a lovable man
beneath that stuffy accountant exterior. All Stephen needed was a
little loosening up!

#887   WILD STREAK—Pat Tracy
Erin Clay had always been off-limits to Linc Severance—first as his
best friend's wife and then as his best friend's widow. Now Linc was
back in town . . . and ready to test the forbidden waters.

#888   YOU MADE ME LOVE YOU—Jayne Addison
Nothing Caroline Phelps ever did seemed to turn out right—*except*
meeting sexy Jack Corey. But when life's little disasters began to
occur, could Caroline trust Jack to always be there?

#889   JUST ONE OF THE GUYS—Jude Randal
Dana Morgan was a do-it-yourself woman—more at home in a
hardware store than in a beauty parlor. But Spencer Willis was out to
prove there *was* one thing Dana couldn't do alone . . . fall in love!

#890   MOLLY MEETS HER MATCH—Val Whisenand
To Molly Evans, Brian Forrester was a gorgeous male specimen. So
what if he was in a wheelchair? But she *couldn't* ignore his stubborn
pride—or his passion . . . even if she wanted to.

#891   THE IDEAL WIFE—Joleen Daniels
Sloan Burdett wanted Lacey Sue Talbert like no woman on earth, but
if he was going to have her, he'd have to move fast. Lacey Sue was
about to walk down the aisle with his brother. . . .

AVAILABLE THIS MONTH:

#880   BABY SWAP
Suzanne Carey

#881   THE WIFE HE WANTED
Elizabeth August

**#882   HOME IS WHERE THE
HEART IS**
Carol Grace

**#883   LAST CHANCE FOR
MARRIAGE**
Sandra Paul

#884   FIRE AND SPICE
Carla Cassidy

**#885   A HOLIDAY TO
REMEMBER**
Brittany Young

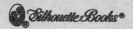

NORA ROBERTS

Love has a language all its own, and for centuries, flowers have symbolized love's finest expression. Discover the language of flowers—and love—in this romantic collection of 48 favorite books by bestselling author Nora Roberts.

Two titles are available each month at your favorite retail outlet.

In August, look for:

Tempting Fate, **Volume #13**
From this Day, **Volume #14**

In September, look for:

All the Possibilities, **Volume #15**
The Heart's Victory, **Volume #16**

Collect all 48 titles and become fluent in

THE LANGUAGE of LOVE

Silhouette®

Silhouette
ROMANCE™